Because of You

Defying her parents by marrying Adam, a white man, Jill Stone believed love could conquer all. And throughout Adam's rise as an executive in a large New York advertising agency, Jill bottled up her unhappiness about his long hours and many trips out of town. But when their sizzling love life fizzled, she couldn't keep quiet anymore. She wanted him home. More. And in her bed.

Adam recognized his marriage was going down the tubes, but couldn't exorcise the demons of Jill's parents thinking he wasn't good enough for her, and the fear that he might somehow end up a failure like his father. He had to succeed. At all costs. To compound his problems, his latest boss was a gorgeous blonde who took one look at Adam's buff, six foot-two body and didn't make any bones about wanting him. Anyway she could get him.

CANDY CAINE

ALSO BY CANDY CAINE

Dancing for Dollars, Flavor of the Week, Softly, As I Leave You,
For the Love of Money, Heated Pleasures, More Heated Pleasures,
Never is Not Forever, Justify My Love, Save the Last Dance for Me
Chasing Rainbows, At First Sight, Honor Most Profane,
Forever Yours, No Strings Attached, A Bridge to Love
For Your Love
It's Love That Really Counts
Crazy Love

PRAISE FOR CANDY CAINE

The Reconstruction of Carla Millhouse ★★★✩✩

"What would you do and how far would you go for love? With great wit, twists and turns, a cast of well- crafted characters you'll want to cheer for, (and some you won't), Candy Caine's delightful story asks and answers this age-old question."

—Niambi Brown Davis, Author of *Sanctuary*

The Reconstruction of Carla Millhouse ★★★✩✩

"A sexy, fabulous read. I couldn't put it down. I was disappointed that the book ended when it did. I could have read on."

—Bertrice Small, Best-selling author of *SKYE O'Malley*

CANDY CAINE
BECAUSE OF YOU

Chapter One

The shifting of her husband's body on the mattress woke Jill Stone in time to catch him getting out of bed. It was her first Saturday off from work in months and she'd hoped they'd be spending it together.

"Come back to bed soon," she whispered, focusing on his delectable tight ass as he walked with nonchalant grace toward the bathroom. Jill was definitely ready for some good morning loving.

Adam stopped and turned to face her. She felt the heat in her body rise as she took in his enticing morning erection. "Can't. I'm heading into the office today."

Jill groaned disappointedly. "Not today of all days."

"Why not? Somebody's got to make a decent living."

That remark wounded Jill on so many levels. The very fact that Adam chose to work rather than spend some quality time with her was bad enough. But his insinuation that she didn't help pull her own weight made her feel insignificant.

All remnants of sleep had been swept away and Jill was now wide awake—and steaming. Her amber-colored eyes narrowed. "That's an unfair remark."

"Really? Do you honestly think we could survive on your salary alone?"

"I don't want to get into an argument. All I want is for us to do something *together* for a change."

"Didn't we sleep together last night?"

"If you meant in the same bed, yeah," she said with cold sarcasm.

Adam ignored what she'd said. "Why wouldn't I go into work today?"

"Because it's Saturday and the first one that I have off in such a long time. Most people don't work on Saturday unless they really have to. And I doubt you really have to—"

Adam thrust out his hand to stop her. "Please don't start that tired old argument with me today, Jill. I'm not in the mood to hear how unfulfilled you feel."

"It wasn't my intention to argue." Jill's voice was hoarse with frustration. "All I want is for us to have a modicum of a life together. With me here and you always at the office, we have hardly a marriage, let alone a life."

"You know I'm doing this for us—"

"Do I? That argument's just as old and worn-out. Maybe it sufficed early in our marriage when you had just started your job and you felt you had to prove yourself, but now that you've accomplished so much...I don't think so."

Jill watched the expression on Adam's handsome face quickly change from annoyance to anger. That he didn't know she'd feel this way was simply mind-boggling. And how long did he actually think the *I'm-doing-this-all-for-you* line would make everything all right? Perhaps if she were a naïve child. However, she was a grown woman with real needs and desires.

"I don't believe you just said that, Jill," Adam replied, a critical tone to his voice.

"Why not? You're not married to me anymore. I've been replaced by your precious advertising accounts."

Adam stiffened as if Jill had struck him and shot her one last penetrating icy-blue look before finally entering the bathroom.

Jill watched him disappear behind the door and lay back down. As tears welled in her eyes, she felt irritated and unhappy with herself for allowing Adam to draw her into another argument. She didn't want to cry and certainly didn't want Adam to see her tears. She was done crying over him and the loneliness he left her to suffice as a companion during all the long, empty evenings. He just didn't comprehend how she felt, and she saw no way to reach him. They just went round and round on a merry-go-round of miscommunication.

At least she knew that it was his work and not another woman that kept him from her. Perhaps if it were another woman, she could fight her...

Adam walked out of the bathroom and picked up the argument where they'd left off. "You're acting ridiculous," he said in a tone one would use when speaking to a child.

"I'm ridiculous?" His remark grated on her, causing her anger to bubble once more to the surface.

"Can't you, for just one moment, look at things through my eyes? Put yourself in my shoes and take a real good look around you. How do you think we've managed to buy all this? It's because of my dedication to my work and the solid hours I give to it," Adam said, as he swept his hand around him for emphasis before thumping his thumb against his chest. "*I* worked my ass off to give you all this."

However, it was the expression on his face that said it all. The tightening of his jaw and the faint pulse to the nerve on the side of his forehead silently shouted out his anger with her selfish attitude. His narrowed blue eyes glared at her like bits of stone. She knew that the conversation was over. Nothing was ever discussed beyond this point. Whenever Adam felt threatened, he shut down, ending any further discussion. By doing so, they never resolved anything and merely left another gaping wound in their marriage. One day they'd run out of Band-Aids to cover those open sores.

"Adam?"

"What is it *now*?" he said through perfect, white, clenched teeth.

Realizing it would be futile to try to reach him at this point, Jill murmured, "Never mind."

She slipped back down into the bed and turned over to face the wall. Tears of frustration and anger began to refill her eyes. She refused to let him see how upset she truly was.

Jill listened as he put on his shoes and left the room. Then several minutes later, she heard the front door open and close, followed by the sound of his car engine starting. Adam was gone. Perhaps he'd be home around dinnertime—perhaps not. At that moment, Jill hardly cared. She was too miserable.

As she lay there sobbing in the silence of her bedroom, Jill thought back to how things used to be in the early years of their marriage. It seemed like so long ago, but it had only been eight years.

She and Adam, like any other newly married couple, had been terribly in love and practically inseparable. It was as if they could never get enough of each other. She would be at her teller's job at the bank watching the clock with one eye and counting the minutes until she could rush home to be enfolded in his loving arms. She'd always find him there waiting to make love to her. Half the time, they hardly made it to the bedroom. Where had all that love and passion gone?

Jill hugged herself as the memory of years past gently drifted through her mind...

They were celebrating their one-month anniversary of being together. Adam had gotten home first and had been waiting for her. He opened the door to their apartment and just seeing him standing there caused a surge of excitement to rush through her. As he swept her into his arms, his nearness made her senses spin. And when his lips hungrily covered hers, she felt a delicious shudder heat her body. Her purse fell to the floor, quickly followed by her coat.

His lips seared a path down her neck and shoulders, eliciting a low moan from her. She eagerly responded with her own feverish kisses. Her restless hands, needing to touch him, threaded their fingers through his thick, blond hair and slipped under his shirt, feeling the smooth texture of his hard back.

Adam had opened her blouse and kissed the swells of her breasts. Hungrily, he reclaimed her mouth. They began to slowly make their way to the bedroom. Clothing dropped as they kissed and bumped their way there. By the time they fell onto the bed with Adam straddling her, they were naked. Jill loved that feeling of skin on skin and had insufficient words to describe what it did to her.

Jill was halfway to heaven by the time Adam entered her. With their hearts hammering in their chests almost beating as one, a sense of urgency dictated their movement. Within moments, Jill's world exploded into a myriad of vibrant colors as noises of pleasure filled the room.

The memory faded and tears of disappointment filled Jill's eyes as she wondered once more, where had all that passion gone?

Jill traced her unhappiness back to that one day following their honeymoon when Adam had gotten out of bed and decided to become God's gift to advertising. He set his sights on becoming his agency's director of client services, which was the person in charge of the entire account service team. From that day on, he was transformed into a workaholic.

The effort paid off for him, which she couldn't deny. He worked hard and in short time became an account director, responsible for two important accounts. Six months later, two more accounts were added. Within three years, he held the title of group account director and was responsible for a group of accounts and had other account directors working under him.

The bonuses and commissions he made were intoxicating, but like any drug, they only served to whet his appetite. He desired to sell more. And like any drug, the more money he made, the more he wanted.

At first Jill thought it was all so very wonderful. She couldn't be any more proud of, and happy for, Adam. They were able to move to the suburbs and buy a beautiful home, one that she'd hoped to fill with children. She also thought that once Adam had established himself, he'd have more time to spend at home and enjoy the fruits of his labor. However, none of this had ever happened.

The reason was simple. Adam was determined to become the director of client services, and because of this, he worked even harder, putting in longer hours at the office. He stopped taking vacations and virtually any time off. Jill couldn't remember the last time they'd spent two consecutive days together.

Having been replaced by his new mistress, work, Jill tried to tell him how lonely she felt. Either her complaint fell on deaf ears or Adam was too consumed by his job to listen. Perhaps he was too selfish to place her needs above his. Whatever the reason, this discussion would nearly always lead to an argument.

Jill assumed this drive to succeed, which propelled Adam to work incessantly, had to do with his dad being an alcoholic who wasn't able to hold a job very long. That would explain Adam's need to achieve. He feared becoming like his father. And he certainly proved her parents wrong.

Her parents, middle-class African Americans, looked down on Adam and his family. To them, he was white trash who'd most likely end up no better than his father. They wanted her to marry a black man and had had several picked out for her. But a handsome, blond, blue-eyed Teutonic god of a man named Adam had come into her life and simply swept her off her feet. And the rest, as they say, was history.

Adam's solution for her loneliness was far from what Jill had envisioned or desired. He suggested she find a hobby to fill her time. However, she didn't want or need a hobby. What she needed was a full-time husband who cared about her and her happiness. One who was at home more than doing God-knows-what at work.

Along with everything else, their once wonderful sexual relationship had gone missing. When Adam came home from work he was usually way too tired to even think about being intimate. It would seem that his career was far more important to him than Jill. It hadn't been long before she grew to hate his job and its intrusion on their lives.

Chapter Two

The week stretched out interminably for Jill. *Find a hobby*, Adam had told her over and over again. He thought that was the solution to all her problems. It wasn't *their* problem, because he found nothing wrong with their marriage. She simply had too much time on her hands and too few time management skills to deal with it. To Adam, Jill was being ridiculous and unreasonable—or worse, needy.

Adam simply blamed her job. Her working in a bank skewed her understanding of the bigger picture. Being in the fishbowl atmosphere of a small bank didn't allow her to appreciate the big, wide world outside of its confines. Sometimes she wondered if he even thought she had a functioning brain.

It wasn't as if Jill hadn't considered taking up a hobby. She had. Nothing seemed to interest her. She hated to sew or knit. And cooking was out. Adam, strictly a meat and potatoes kind of guy, would never appreciate any new dishes. She'd end up eating her own masterpieces and turn into a backup replacement for the Goodyear Blimp or, God forbid, on a weight-loss reality show.

"A hobby is not what I need," Jill muttered aloud. "*What I do need is a more attentive husband*," she said pushing every word through a clenched jaw.

As she stepped out of the shower stall and began to towel herself off, she caught a glimpse of her reflection in the full-length mirror. What she saw did not make her happy. She finished drying off her smooth, caramel colored skin, studying her entire body carefully. It looked as if she'd put on some weight, and it wasn't in places that flattered her figure. That would explain why her clothes were beginning to feel snug.

Jill sighed. Maybe it was time to join a gym. Her job as a bank teller wasn't helping. Seated behind a window keying numbers into a computer was not much exercise. Her sister, Lynne, who lived in

Arizona, swore by her gym membership and loved her personal trainer, Joey, with whom she scheduled maintenance sessions every so often. And from the way her husband, Haywood, looked at Lynne, he definitely appreciated her toned, petite body.

Jill sat down in front of her make-up table and pulled the towel off her long, dark-brown hair. Brushing it as she used the blow dryer, she thought further about the gym idea and pooh-poohed it. She'd hated sports in school, and if she signed up for the gym, she'd probably go a few times and then let her membership lapse. Perhaps, if she watched what she ate and did more walking, she'd be able to shed those extra pounds.

***

Adam was late for dinner. *What a surprise*, Jill thought sarcastically as she curled up on the den sofa and booted up her Kindle to the story she'd been reading. She might even finish the book while she waited for "his highness" to come home.

A little voice inside her head chastised her for her attitude. It would only press the wrong buttons and start another argument like the doozy they'd had on Saturday. That was the last thing she needed. She wanted peace and harmony. But most of all, she desired to return to the days when they couldn't keep their hands off one another. Just thinking about it made her horny.

***

As Adam sat on the train taking him home from Manhattan to Locust Valley, an upscale suburb on Long Island, he thought about the arguments he and Jill had been having frequently over the long hours he'd been putting in at work. He knew she was lonely, but there was little he could do to change that.

So many times he wanted to tell her about how stressful his job had become. When he had first joined Roberts, White and Gould Advertising Agency, the firm felt like a second home. The CEO, Joseph Roberts, had taken Adam under his wing, obviously having detected his potential. During that time Adam worked his butt off and was rewarded with handsome raises as he rose from the rank of account manager to account director and eventually a group account director. He was definitely on the fast track to becoming the director of client services.

Unfortunately, Joseph Roberts succumbed to a heart attack and died. The agency continued without Roberts for nearly a year before the economy took a downturn and revenues fell. White and Gould sold the agency to Hartford Advertising, a larger, more global agency.

Everything changed with the sale of the company. Things became very volatile. The director of client services was let go, along with several other account directors. Even though Adam was spared, more stress was added to an already tense situation. The new director of client services was a ball buster and constantly on Adam's back to speed up the timelines of projects and bring more revenue into the agency. Fortunately, that guy had lasted only several months, but during those months, he'd expected one hundred and twenty percent from Adam and his team of account directors, which had been decimated.

It was as if Adam had to prove himself all over again. It was his responsibility to ensure that all the work for over a dozen accounts was completed on time and within budget. It was his head on the chopping block if the clients weren't happy.

With the economy so sluggish, most companies had to cut their spending. Advertising was the first expense item to go, and the agency was feeling the pinch. People who had been there as long as he were being let go. For a long while, when he walked in each day, he felt his guts liquefy, wondering if it was his turn to receive a pink slip.

Adam was taught by his father it was a sign of weakness to tell anyone—especially women—of your flaws. "Never tell your problems to a woman, boy. They'll just use them to emasculate and eat you alive," his daddy had said. And lately things with Jill hadn't been so hot. So, he'd told her none of what was happening at work. There was no way he'd want to worry her or have her think of him as anything less than a success. He'd rather die than lose his job and fulfill her parents' low expectations of him. Therefore, he kept all his apprehensions about work to himself.

It mattered little to Jill's parents that he had provided their daughter with a beautiful home in an affluent area of Long Island, because they'd never forgiven him from taking her away from them and her culture. To them, Adam was white trailer trash and would remain so. They'd tarred him with the same brush as his father, an alcoholic, who couldn't seem to hold a job for long. Adam was worthless in their eyes and they never turned down a chance to let him know it.

How could he even hint to Jill his job had been in jeopardy? There was no way. He loved Jill, but blamed her attitude on her parents, who he felt had filled her pretty head with unrealistic expectations about marriage. Adam was doing everything he could to make her happy. But, unfortunately, he was human and not a superman. And he doubted that those black guys her parents had hand-picked for Jill were, either.

Chapter Three

Jill had always loved to read as a child, so she merely continued to do just that as an adult. She devoured one romance book after another. It was a poor substitute for everything she felt was lacking in her own life, unless she was happy having sex once or twice a month— if she was lucky. Reading allowed her to escape reality for a brief time and vicariously live the life and loves of the heroines. It wasn't too different from when she was a child and craved her mother's love. Too bad the woman had just enough for herself and her causes. Many times Jill and her sister, Lynne, had to raid the refrigerator for dinner.

However, Jill didn't consider reading to be a hobby—at least not in the classic sense like sewing or scrapbooking. So despite her outward reluctance, she continually searched for something more that she could tailor to her needs. Something that would sustain her interest longer than a few days and get her creative juices flowing. Perhaps something that would make Adam stop and take interest.

She wasn't certain when the idea first began to germinate in her mind, but after having read her zillionth romance, and disappointed with the ending, she found herself thinking of an alternate one. Realizing what she was doing, it occurred to her that she should try to write her own book. *Why not?* After all, she had nothing to lose. So Jill decided to write her own romance novel.

And from that moment on, she became a lady with a mission. She had given herself a goal and would stop at nothing to achieve it. With Adam away from home so much, she felt as if she had all the time in the world to pursue this dream—and pursue it, she would.

***

Knowing absolutely nothing about the technique of writing, Jill went to the library after work and picked up several books on the subject to get her feet wet. That night she read way into the wee hours. By the time she had to shower and dress for work, Jill was hooked. She truly wanted to write.

The next day after work, she marched into the Apple store and purchased a laptop. Adam had a computer at home, but she wanted her own. And honestly, she felt more comfortable keeping her writing plans a secret—especially from him. That way, if she failed and didn't complete a book, there would be no embarrassment.

With her new computer safely stowed in the trunk of her Sonata, she drove home excited about her new venture. In fact, there was so much excitement bubbling inside her that it nearly made her giddy. The feeling reminded her of Christmases past when she was a child about to open her first present. She could hardly wait to set up her new laptop.

This idea of writing and creating a story that could transport people into the time and place of her choosing was quickly becoming a passion—a vehicle into which she could channel all her needs and desires. And it made her feel good—really good.

Chapter Four

Over the next several months, Jill read every how-to book she could get her hands on and soon discovered there was much more to writing than putting words to paper. It was quite a process that didn't end even after she wrote a compelling story. She still needed to find a publisher willing to take a chance on a newcomer. Then she would work with an editor to polish the novel before it got published. After publication, the novel would begin the marketing part of the journey. And with all the self-publishing going on and so many people trying their hand at writing, promoting the book became extremely important. Promotion was done mainly by the author, but if the author was lucky, the publisher participated, as well.

Jill realized that it was one thing to have the desire to write a book, but it was another thing to come up with a sustainable plotline. Her mind was filled with dozens of ideas, but none seemed to resonate within her. Even so, she wrote all these ideas down on a yellow pad. She knew that a special plotline would move her and rock her world and hopefully engage her readers, as well.

The idea for her novel came to her early one morning as she stepped into the shower. She recalled an old story her mother used to love to recount about her great great grandparents. They had been in love, but since they were slaves they had been separated when each was sold. They never stopped searching for each other and for a way for them to be together. It was a romantic, powerful story. Maybe she could use it as a basis for a novel. Even the title that came to her was appropriate: *Never Leave Me*. She repeated it over and over again in her head. It was perfect.

***

Jill had become passionate about her writing. She tried to find the time to write whenever she could, by getting up early each morning before work and then writing as much as she could during her lunch hour. Not wanting Adam to find out about her writing, she was only able to write when he wasn't at home. When she received her local library's program brochure in the mail, it gave her an idea. She could tell Adam she'd joined the Great Books Discussion Group that met every Wednesday and have an excuse to leave his dinner in the fridge, freeing her up to write at the library. What could be more perfect than that? Okay, it was a lie, but only a little white one. She could live with that. And if she never finished her novel or couldn't get it published, it would never matter.

There were two other young women working at the bank who were around Jill's age. Renee MacKay was a strikingly tall, curvy redhead whose boobs got to her station a good five seconds before the rest of her. Doreen Bossey, a cherub-faced, sweet-talking, African American with a humdinger of a southern accent, seemed to be able to charm most of the men into opening special accounts. At twenty-eight, Jill was the oldest and the only married one.

And she seemed to be the only woman in that shift who didn't have a wild and crazy life outside the bank. Renee and Doreen had no qualms about discussing the men they met and slept with. From the way they talked, it was obvious to Jill that the girls thought being married was a license to nonstop sexual debauchery. *If they only knew.*

At first Jill was a little jealous of their sexual antics, but listening to them became fodder for her novel. Of course, she could never tell them she was writing one. Therefore, if they saw her doing any writing on her lunch hour, she once again used the excuse of writing a critique on the book she was reading for the Great Books Discussion Group from the library. The girls teased her about being a bookworm, but left her alone to write.

The only person Jill confided in was her sister, Lynne. When Jill first mentioned she was writing a romance novel during a phone call, Lynne's reaction was classic. "You're finally writing a 'tell all' about our crazy, dysfunctional family?"

"Didn't you catch the word *romance* in what I just said?"

"Now that you mention it, yeah, I did. That would definitely exclude our *loving* parents. But tell me, are you really serious about writing, Jill?"

"Cardiac-arrest serious."

"Throwing around big words already— I guess you are. Seriously, Sis, I think it's great."

"Honest to God?" Jill asked.

"Cross my heart, honest. You know I love you and wish you only the best. So go for it! And I'll be the first person ion line to buy the book."

Jill knew her younger sister would be her most ardent fan. Born eleven months apart, they had been so close growing up. While their parents were marching to improve the welfare of African Americans in the United States, their two daughters were left in the care of their paternal grandmother, who had a fondness for alcohol. Unfortunately for Jill and Lynne, Granny was often found sprawled out cold in her rocker in front of the TV by four in the afternoon. If they wanted to eat, they had to fend for themselves.

While their parents were actively pouring their time, hearts, and souls into furthering African American causes, their own children, Jill and Lynne, had managed to disappoint them in the worst possible way by marrying white men. Mr. and Mrs. Daniels didn't believe in the adage that love is blind. In fact, when Jill told them she was getting married to Adam, the scene that took place in the kitchen of their small apartment in Trenton could have been a pivotal scene right out of a movie.

Jill had had the foresight not to bring Adam around to meet her parents until she had paved the way first. She knew it wouldn't be easy, but damn, she didn't think she'd need a backhoe. Her father exploded and nearly had a stroke, while her mother fell to her knees sobbing, "Where did I go wrong, sweet Jesus?"

There had been no way she could explain to them how much she loved Adam. It had truly been love at first sight. It had been love, not God, that had worked in mysterious ways. And love is definitely blind. It doesn't see the color of one's skin. When those pheromones hit you, you're a goner.

When the tall, handsome, blond man wearing a blue pinstripe suit approached her window at the bank, it was as if the hero from her Viking story had just time traveled out of the romance novel she was currently reading and walked into her bank. She envisioned the broad-shouldered body under the blue suit with a muscle-toned torso tapering to his waist. Jill felt her mouth grow dry as her eyes focused on his sensual lips as he spoke. Though all he asked her to do was cash his check, those few words were music to her ears. He thanked her as she gave him the money and managed to say, "you're welcome." Then he was gone.

As her heartbeat began to slow, Jill realized how silly she'd been, since she'd never see that gorgeous guy named Adam Stone again. Her eyes had nearly devoured the name on the check. It was a wonder they'd left no scorch marks. Of course she had no idea that the love bug had stung Mr. Adam Stone just as hard.

He came back the following day to cash another check. Again, Jill felt her heart ping pong against the walls of her chest as he approached. "Hello, Ms. Daniels," was all he said, and her insides began to liquefy. "I need to cash this check. I also have a favor to ask of you."

Her heart was pumping so much blood; she could hardly hear the man's voice over the noise. "Favor? We don't give out samples in this bank."

The Viking god gave out a throaty chuckle. "I'm in town for a few days on business and have no one to have lunch with. If I promise to be on my best behavior, would you meet me for lunch at the Italian restaurant across the street?"

Jill couldn't say no, and that lunch had led to dinner. By the end of dinner, she knew she was crazy in love with Mr. Adam Stone from New York. Their flame of love burned so brightly that they decided to get married six months later. She gave notice to the bank and married Adam in front of the justice of the peace. The only person present was Lynne and a guy that Adam worked with named Scott Breyer. Of course her parents never showed. Why would they? They had never accepted Adam. To them he was an embarrassment.

After Jill married Adam and moved to New York, Lynne couldn't bear to listen to her parents go on and on about their stupid daughter and how she had betrayed her people and her race. Her parents had turned love into a race crime. Lynne had had enough of their rancor and decided to move to Phoenix. It had been a bold step, but she had applied for a real estate job that would help her obtain a license. There she met Haywood Wish and fell in love. When Lynne married Haywood, also white, the Daniels were all but devastated. Of course, they blamed Lynne's marriage on Jill, but still cut Lynne no slack. Both daughters were stricken from their wills.

Because Jill trusted Lynne's advice, she used her as a sounding board. She'd often discuss her book with her, bouncing off ideas and asking advice whenever she got stuck. Lynne understood why she hadn't told Adam about her secret project and promised to keep it to herself.

***

Now, nearly eight months later, Jill felt that her story, *Never Leave Me*, was finished, self-edited, and ready to be sent out into the world. She knew the hardest part would be to find a prominent publishing house willing to read her manuscript. Most of the large New York–based houses didn't accept non-agented work, so she decided her best avenue to break into publishing would be to acquire an agent. She'd researched those agencies looking for new clients and picked out an agency that was seeking stories similar to hers.

After saying a silent prayer, Jill emailed a query letter containing the first three chapters of her completed novel and a synopsis, or detailed plotline, to a prominent New York agency, hoping they'd want to read the rest of her story. She immediately called Lynne who wished her luck and then it was off to bed.

Adam was sound asleep when Jill slipped under the blanket. She wished she could tell him that she had written a book and had sent it out to an agent. It would be nice to have him hold her hand in support as she waited to hear back from the agency, but Adam was so wrapped up in his career that she doubted he would care. Yet he'd have to know if her book was ever sold. *What a nice ring those words had*, she thought. Lynne had said to her on the phone earlier, "I think it's time to tell Adam, Jill." Maybe she was right.

***

When Jill got home from work two weeks after sending her query, she immediately checked her email, as she did every day, hoping for a response from the agency. Slowly she scrolled down the list of e-mails and noticed that the agency had responded. She took a deep breath before opening the message. *Yes!* They had requested the entire manuscript. Excitedly, and now truly hopeful, she attached her novel in its entirety to her reply, saying a little prayer before she clicked send. Assuring herself that there were many more agents to try if this agency turned her down, she made dinner for Adam and hoped he would show up before it was overcooked and as tasty as shoe leather.

Adam surprised Jill by being on time that night. Over dinner Jill got up the courage and casually mentioned that she'd written a novel and that an agent was interested in it. Adam was filling his mouth with mashed potatoes and nearly choked. After gulping down water to clear his throat, he managed to squeak, "You wrote a novel?"

"Why are you so surprised?"

"Well, this is the first I'm hearing of it. Why shouldn't I be surprised?"

"Can't you be happy for me? Not everybody finishes a book."

"Writing a book is one thing, but selling it and getting it into print is another," Adam said sipping some more water.

Thanks for the support, Jill thought wondering why she bothered to tell him in the first place.

***

Three days later, while Jill was on her lunch break at work, she received the call from Joan Wilson of the Slattery Book Agency. She loved the book and her agency wanted to represent Jill! When Jill agreed, the woman faxed the paperwork to the bank where Jill worked. Much to Jill's surprise, Ms. Wilson had wanted to get the process started ASAP.

Excitedly, Jill called Adam to tell him about the great news. In less than three minutes, he pricked her balloon of happiness, and again she wondered why she even bothered to call him in the first place.

"Sounds good, Jill, but getting someone to represent you is not actually selling the book. When the book is sold and in print, then it'll be time to celebrate," he said abstractedly.

Thanks for your feel-good speech, she mused as her bubbly mood fizzled. Suddenly a knot of rage that had begun deep within her shot to the surface. It was as if Adam's words had hit an exposed nerve. "Then be prepared to celebrate. My novel will be sold—I just know it!"

"Okay, okay. Good luck with that. I'll see you tonight."

It took a beat or two for Jill to realize he'd hung up. "Great," she said aloud to herself. "Thanks for the support, Adam."

To make herself feel better, she called Lynne to tell her the news.

***

Jill was still upset by Adam's nonchalant attitude on the phone by the time she'd left work that day, but she was proud that she had been able to finish the book and decided she wasn't going to allow him to rain on her parade.

When Adam came home she didn't bring up the subject of her book. Obviously he'd forgotten all about it, as well, because he made no reference to it. She kept her bruised feelings inside and went to bed early. The last conscious thought she had was that completing the book and signing with an agent was truly an achievement—no matter what anybody thought.

***

Nearly two months later, Joan Wilson called Jill. Even though the woman sounded upbeat, Jill, remembering Adam's words, didn't get her hopes up about having her book sold.

"Are you sitting down, Jill?"

"Actually, I am."

"Good. Because I have the most wonderful news to tell you."

"Did a publishing company offer to buy my book?" Jill asked, suddenly finding it hard to breathe.

Joan Wilson actually giggled. "I'd say so. I just got you a three-book deal with an advance of $20,000."

"What? How? Really?" Jill's words came out in a rush as one.

"You, my girl, are on the way to being the next best-selling novelist."

"I...I...I'm speechless. How is that possible?"

Joan Wilson laughed. "Our agency went gaga over your manuscript. We knew we had a winner. And so did several publishers."

"Several publishers?"

"Yup. They bid for it. Your book is going to be hotter than hot."

"So, which company will be publishing my book?"

"Sorry. I did manage to leave that essential fact out, didn't I? It's Barnaby and Sons."

"Wow! They're big! Aren't they?"

"Yup. One of the biggest."

"Umm...What do I do now?"

Joan Wilson laughed. "You're going to meet your editor on Friday afternoon—if you're free."

"Free? Tell me where and when," Jill replied.

"Slow down, girl, or else you'll self-destruct before Friday. There's a place called Bar American on 52nd Street. We'll all meet there, say around one o'clock."

"That's fine. Do I need to bring anything?"

"Nope. Just yourself."

"Looking forward to it," Jill said as the phone call ended and she tried to slow her heartbeat down. She could have sworn it was doing backflips in her rib cage.

Chapter Five

Jill's mind raced nearly the entire night before the meeting. She knew she was being silly, but first impressions were so important and she wanted to give her agent and editor a good one. She picked out her best suit to wear, making certain her purse and shoes matched perfectly. Even so, she was still nervous. It reminded her of her first job interview and how she had stuttered and sounded like a total idiot. Hopefully, she wouldn't repeat history.

***

Joan Wilson was waiting in front of the Bar American restaurant when Jill emerged from the taxi she'd taken from Penn Station. Joan didn't need to hold up a sign that read *agent*, because she looked every bit the part of one. She was a tall woman with shoulder-length dark hair, dressed in a tailored, blue suit, holding a leather messenger bag. Jill guessed the woman to be in her early thirties.

Jill walked up to her and said, "Hello. By any chance are you Joan Wilson?"

A warm smile appeared on the woman's face and she extended her hand. "Hello, Jill, I'm so glad to meet you."

"Hey! You two! Don't start eating without me!"

A moment later, a short fireplug of a woman with light-brown hair, approximately Jill's age, came huffing and puffing to meet them. She was toting a large book bag that was almost as big as her.

"Hello, Robin," Joan said. "This is Jill Stone. Jill, this is your editor, Robin Wycoff."

Suddenly, Robin grabbed Jill and hugged her to her ample bosom, nearly deflating her lungs. "Boy, am I glad to meet you," she told Jill, who didn't have to live in the borough of Brooklyn to recognize the fact that Robin came from there.

After being released, Jill replied, "Me, too."

Joan had watched with amusement. She suggested, "Let's go inside and have some lunch."

The inside of the restaurant resembled a bar with tables filled with patrons. Knowing how busy the place usually got, Joan had reserved a table. The women were seated and the waiter presented them with menus. Jill was still filled with nervous excitement and had nearly no appetite, but ordered the plate of the day, which was snapper, steamed in parchment. Joan ordered a Cobb salad and Robin a steak. All three women had the Vidalia onion soup as an appetizer.

During the meal Robin explained the process of how Jill's book would be published. "I intend to work very closely with you Jill, editing the manuscript. During this time, the creative services department will design the cover. Several months before the book gets published, we will start promoting it. By the time the book hits the bookshelves, everyone will be talking about it. That's our goal. We're very excited about your book."

It was nearly 3 o'clock by the time they said goodbye. Joan Wilson was a very nice lady, but Robin Wycoff was a hoot. If she ever gave up editing, she could well become a standup comic.

***

The next several weeks of Jill's life centered around editing and doing rewrites of her novel. She worked very closely with Robin and often discussed the edits on the telephone as well as through e-mails. There were times when she nearly forgot to make dinner for Adam. Even though he wasn't always on time, he expected dinner to be waiting for him. However, Jill got so wrapped up with the edits that she was often unaware of the time. Sometimes, she even took off from work to work on them.

When Jill saw the cover of her novel for the first time with her name on it, her heart swelled with pride. It represented her unique achievement. For the first time in her life, Jill felt important. She was a somebody—not Adam's wife or her parents' daughter. She wasn't walking in someone's shadow, she was casting her own.

And she couldn't wait to hold the book.

"What are you doing?" Adam said as he walked into the kitchen. "You haven't even started dinner."

"Oh, my gosh! What time is it?"

"Six o'clock."

"Sorry. I lost track of time. I'll order some Chinese. Want anything special?"

"No. Get what you want," he said angrily.

"Look, I'm really sorry, but—"

"I know. The edits."

"Look! I've got the cover of the book," she said showing him.

"Nice. Order the food. I'm going to wash up."

Jill watched Adam walk away. He could've been a little excited for her. Then again, lately he'd been so distracted and tonight was no different. She wondered what was wrong—not that he'd tell her. Sometimes she wondered why he kept everything so bottled up inside him. Why couldn't they communicate anymore? *Because he always puts his career ahead of us. It sucks all the time and energy out of him. No wonder little is left for us.*

***

Adam went upstairs into the bathroom and leaned over the sink. He looked into the mirror. The man staring back at him look tired. He was beat. The job was getting to him. The new director of client services, Charles Aloe, turned out to be a major prick. For some reason he resented Adam and seemed to live with the desire to make Adam miserable. Always looking over Adam's shoulder, it seemed as if he wanted Adam to screw up. He'd often countermand a decision Adam made and then expected Adam to repair the damage.

At this point, Adam was ready to jump ship. Unfortunately, it wasn't a very good time to do so. He was fortunate he still had a high-paying job in today's economy. Therefore Adam found himself treading water, hoping that the market would have an upswing before he went under.

That morning, Adam had been called into Charles Aloe's office. It was soon evident the purpose was to ream Adam a new one.

"Revenues are down this month, Stone. I expected them to increase at best and remain the same at worst. If you can't make that happen, I'll find somebody who can."

Adam truly desired to belt this guy into the next office, but he said nothing. He wouldn't give the man any reason to fire him. He only wished somebody upstairs would recognize the man for what he was—an asshole.

"Go on, Stone. Try to get something accomplished."

Adam had walked out of Aloe's office feeling angry and frustrated. His entire day had been ruined.

He at least expected to find some comfort at home with a loving, supportive wife. Did his home life have to suck, as well? Dinner could've been ready for him. Was that so much to expect?

Chapter Six

The pre-promotion of *Because of You* was now in full-court-press mode, and the first of the reviews were coming in. Jill's heart virtually sang when she read each and every one of them. She'd prepared herself for any negative ones that came her way—or at least tried her best to, but it had been unnecessary. They were mainly five-star songs of praise. She was depicted as "the new kid on the block" and the "one author to read before anyone else." If she were to believe all the hype—and she wanted to—her book seemed destined to be a success. Still...she nervously waited for the other shoe to drop.

Robin Wycoff called her. "Have you been catching the reviews, kiddo?"

"Yes. I can't believe how incredible they are. Beginner's luck?"

"Nope. Fantastic book. We're so excited here. Your book could be a bestseller."

"How I wish."

"If the reviews are any indication, you might just get your wish. Well, gotta run. My stomach's grumbling."

Jill laughed. "Enjoy lunch. Speak to you soon."

"Thanks to you, I will."

Jill put her cell away and went back to her station. She felt terrific. Her novel would be published soon, and then perhaps it would be real enough to pass Adam's stringent criteria. She could hardly wait to see his face in a week or so when it went to print and he held the book. Maybe then he'd be more supportive.

***

That following day, Adam had every intention of coming home on time again. He always felt worn out lately. Work had become so stressful that he sometimes wished they would fire him, even though he realized that telling Jill would be worse.

Unfortunately, Adam's day took a downward turn from the moment he walked through the glass doors of his agency. And good intentions were the only thing he had going for him. He'd just had time to make it to his desk when his intercom buzzed.

It was Susan Smith, the administrative assistant to Roy Jackson, CEO and one of the managing partners of the Hartford Advertising Agency, letting him know that he was being summoned upstairs. Immediately, Adam's heart jumped into his throat. Perhaps Charles had finally gotten his desire to get Adam canned. Doomsday scenarios started to play in Adam's mind. What would he do? Jill mustn't know. And if her parents ever found out...

"Adam? Are you still there?"

"Yes, of course. I'm on my way."

Like a condemned man taking his last walk to his place of execution, Adam took the elevator up two floors. The piped-in music seemed more annoying than usual. The doors opened, and he proceeded down the hall and through the glass door to Susan Smith's desk.

"He's waiting for you. Go right inside," she said, buzzing Jackson.

Roy Jackson, a trim, medium-height man in his late fifties, was seated behind his large mahogany desk. His office boasted large windows on two sides, giving him a gorgeous view of the city. The brown carpeting was lush, and the leather couch and matching chairs were expensive-looking. There was a glass case containing several gold Clios, the highest award given for creative advertising. Family pictures dotted the walls and lined a low bookshelf set against a wall.

Adam couldn't tell from the expression on Jackson's tanned, bearded face whether or not he was going to be fired, since Jackson had the best poker face he'd ever seen. It wasn't the firing, but the aftermath, that worried Adam the most. He just wanted to get it over with fast.

"Have a seat," Jackson said gesturing to one of the chairs in front of his desk.

Adam just wanted to stand and get it over with, but complied, choosing the chair on the left of Jackson's desk.

"Joel Fried called me early this morning. He wasn't a very happy man. I was wondering why he chewed my ear off. I thought our advertising campaign with Hudson Food Corp. was on track. Can you please enlighten me as to why Joel Fried, their advertising manager, should be calling me?"

"When I spoke to Fried last week, there wasn't anything wrong. He definitely was happy with the campaign. Honestly, I haven't the faintest idea why he called you."

"According to Fried, he found out from our production department that his thirty-second Super Bowl TV spot was seriously behind schedule due to some 'bullshit technicality.' I called our creative director, and he told me they had to stop production due to cost overruns. What's he talking about? And why wasn't I told there was a problem?"

"This is the first I'm hearing about this, too." Adam frowned, thinking furiously. Production would have informed Charles Aloe, his boss, if there was a problem, and since this was Adam's account, he should have been informed, too. "As far as I knew, production was on schedule. It was imperative that the ad be ready to air during the Super Bowl halftime. We could lose the entire account because of it."

Jackson grimaced. "If it isn't fixed, we will. But I'm truly troubled here. The only other person who might have halted production would have been Charles. By any chance, did production go over budget with Fried's ad? This is your account, Adam."

Adam shook his head. "As far I know, everything is on time and on budget. The outside production crew we hired for this commercial was included in the proposed budget." He realized what Charles had done and was livid. He had to have added unnecessary run costs not included in the original proposal without Adam's knowledge. The Hudson Ford account was Adam's major account. If the account was screwed up, Adam would take the fall. The major question here was, who would Jackson ultimately blame for the fiasco?

"That's what I needed to know. Thanks, Adam."

Adam left and headed back to his office. His throat felt so constricted he could hardly breathe. He opened the top button on his shirt and loosened his tie. He knew Charles Aloe was a snake, but he never expected the man to stoop to undermining the entire company as a way of getting rid of him.

The entire scenario played out in his head. Aloe had planned this carefully. The additional run costs would cause a delay and make Adam look incompetent. The creative director would have told Aloe of the problem and would have had no reason to alert Adam, as well. If Fried hadn't checked up on production, the ad would not have been ready for the Super Bowl.

Adam sighed. If Roy Jackson believed that Adam was derelict in his duties, he would be fired. *Unbelievable!*

As the elevator doors opened on Adam's floor, Charles Aloe was standing there. "On the way to your office to clean out your desk, Stone?"

Adam clenched his jaw. His hands fisted at his sides. It took all of his willpower not to wipe the smirk off Aloe's face. This confirmed what Adam thought.

"I have no idea what you're talking about." Then straightening his shoulders, Adam walked toward his office. He could feel Aloe's eyes boring into his back. Adam heard the elevator doors close as he reached his office.

Opening his desk drawer, Adam took out a bottle of whiskey that he kept for moments like this. He poured himself two fingers and downed it. His head was now throbbing. He felt like a man drowning in frustration, for there was little he could do. He should've walked when he was offered the job a couple years ago with Flanagan and Green, a small up-and-coming agency in California. But he had invested so much of himself into the Hartford Agency who'd believed in him, it didn't seem right. What good was his loyalty to Hartford now? It certainly wasn't going to save him here.

He got up and began to pace. Who was he scheduled to meet with today? Perhaps he should reschedule. No. That would be wrong. Besides, what was he going to do, merely sit here and wait for the axe to fall? The best thing was to get his mind off the situation—as if he could— and keep his appointments with his clients. What did he have to lose? If he ever got a job with another agency, there was always the chance some of these clients would follow him.

***

Jill showered and dressed for work. She felt troubled. Lately, she and Adam seemed to argue more often. They'd become just like her parents, who never shied away from a good fight. The thought soured her stomach. Most of the arguments centered on his erratic work schedule and her writing obligations.

Arguments concerning his job were nothing new. Her writing was. She felt angry and disappointed that Adam didn't support her writing career as much as she'd like. It was almost as if he didn't take it seriously. She wondered if he resented it. Perhaps he thought she was putting her career first? Was Adam still angry with her for forgetting to make dinner that one night?

She loved Adam—of course she did—and yet, they'd become like planets whose orbits crossed one another, but never collided. Perhaps she should take matters into her own hands and attempt to bring back the passion they once shared. It seemed a crying shame that the characters in her book had more sex than she did.

Jill decided to do something positive about that. She would seduce Adam and make him want what he used to hunger for. Tonight was as good a night as ever. The thought alone made her wet with desire.

***

Adam got back to his office by three o'clock. His assistant, Mary, stopped him and pointed upstairs. "He said to send you up the minute you got back."

Again Adam's heart lurched sideways. It wasn't as if his potential firing hadn't been the elephant camping out in his head the entire day, but at least he was on the outside still breathing the air of an employed man. Well, his reprieve was over. *Time to face the music*, he thought as he slowly headed toward the elevator.

Roy Jackson was standing at the window looking out at the city when Adam walked into his office. "You know, Adam, I never tire of looking out this window. It's such a great view. I never thought I'd like living in Manhattan. I'm from Idaho, originally."

"I didn't know that."

Jackson turned and walked back to his desk. "Sit down. We have a great deal to discuss."

***

On her way home from work, Jill turned around on Northern Blvd. and backtracked to the entrance to Northern Parkway. She drove eastbound toward the Roosevelt Field mall. The plan of seduction was gelling in her mind and that brought a smile to her full, pouty lips.

She parked her car in the lot near Macy's. Though the lot was packed, luckily for her someone had pulled out right in front of her as she turned into a lane. Now on a mission, she hurried into the mall, checked the directory, and headed for Victoria's Secret. The store was busy so no one paid her any mind, exactly what she'd wanted. Shopping here wasn't in her normal purview. She made her way to the lingerie area. Looking through stuff that made her blush, she found a sexy black teddy that would show off her ample bosom and high, firm buns—two assets Adam got off on. This teddy would drive him crazy.

Making her way out of the mall, she got back into her car and drove to an adult shop nearby. She swallowed her embarrassment by reminding herself this was for an important cause and entered. A young woman with piercings through her eyebrow, nose, and lips approached her. Her short, shaggy blonde hair had blue stripes running through it. When she asked if she could help Jill find something, Jill noticed the tattoo on her forearm that read: Love Toy.

Jill lied. "I need a gag gift for a friend's shower." She was certain by the expression on the other woman's face that she didn't believe her.

"Do you have something specific in mind?"

"Handcuffs—but not real metal ones."

Blondie gestured with two fingers over her shoulder. "Follow me. I think I have the perfect set."

Jill found herself standing in front of a wall that held rows and rows of packaged handcuffs that looked pretty authentic. The girl directed her attention to the last three rows on the right. There Jill saw handcuffs made of all types of material from tiger fur to plastic. The last thing in the world she wanted to happen was to have to call 911 to open a set of handcuffs because the key had gone missing. With that scenario foremost in her mind, she chose a pair of black sporty cuffs made of soft neoprene and held in place with Velcro. They had never tried bondage before, but the thought of Adam handcuffing her to the bed and spreading her legs wide while he pumped into her was definitely appealing.

When the salesgirl asked, "Anything else?" Jill swallowed hard and said, "I'd also like a vibrator." She knew Adam used to get off on watching her pleasure herself. Watching her run a vibrator over her clit was sure to drive him wild.

The other woman smiled knowingly and brought Jill back to the largest selection of vibrators Jill thought possible. They came in all shapes, sizes, and colors. When the salesgirl saw the expression on Jill's face, she explained how several popular ones worked.

Fifteen minutes later, Jill chose what the woman had called a rabbit-type vibrator. The device, which vibrated and rotated, was in the shape of a phallus with a clitoral stimulator attached to the shaft. She thanked the girl for all her help and paid for the vibrator and handcuffs. Definitely glad her purchases were in a plain nondescript bag, Jill headed for home.

Rush-hour traffic was building, and it was taking longer than she'd expected. She wouldn't have time to make dinner. To solve this problem, she stopped at a supermarket and bought a rotisserie chicken, some ready-made potato salad, coleslaw, and a strawberry shortcake for dessert.

By the time she got home, she was giddy with excitement just thinking about her plans for the evening. She looked at the clock on the microwave. Adam would be home in an hour or so.

She took her purchases upstairs, hiding her vibrator and handcuffs in her nightstand and the teddy on the back of the bathroom door. Boy, was Adam going to be in for it tonight. She rubbed her palms together in delight.

***

When Jackson told Adam to sit down after telling him they had a great deal to discuss, Adam felt like a kid back in school sitting in front of the principal. What was the worst that could happen? Getting fired. No the worst thing was imagining Aloe doing backflips in delight.

"It didn't take me much digging to come up with the truth," Jackson said. "I know who was responsible for the cost overruns, who instructed production to shut down. In fact, I know the entire story, Adam."

Here it comes. Adam felt his throat close as his stomach went into freefall. The tuna sandwich he'd eaten for lunch threatened to resurface.

"I'm sorry you weren't here to see security escort Charles Aloe off the premises. It was quite a spectacle. The lying sack of shit actually tried to pin it on you, but we had him six ways from Sunday."

Adam realized these were not the words he'd been expecting. It took him a moment to internalize them. "I'm glad you know it wasn't me," he replied, relief washing over him.

"Me, too. 'Cause now you have to fly to Buffalo and smooth some very ruffled feathers at Hudson Food. Convince them everything is back on track. The corporate jet will be waiting for you at La Guardia. You're booked into the Hyatt Regency."

Adam nearly groaned aloud. That was the last thing he'd desired to do tonight. "Does Fried expect me?"

"Most definitely. You have a dinner date with him at 8 PM at E. B. Green's in the hotel."

Adam got up to leave and got as far as the door when Jackson stopped him. "And Adam..."

Adam turned around.

"Make the man happy."

Adam took the agency's car service to the airport. He always kept a packed overnight bag at his office for emergencies, so he didn't need to go home to pack. He called Jill on the way.

"Hey, babe," he began.

"Hopefully you're on your way home. I have a surprise for you."

"I do, too, but I have a feeling yours would have been better," he replied.

"What do you mean?"

"I'm on my way to the airport—"

"Damn it, Adam. Why?"

"It's a long story, but the short version is that my boss was canned and I have to save an account."

"The director of client services?"

"Yeah."

"Are you the only capable guy in that agency?"

"Right now, yeah. I'm sorry. I'd rather be home with you."

"Yeah, sure," she said not disguising the disappointment. There went their special night.

"I'm really sorry," Adam said again, but Jill had already hung up. *If she only knew the half of what I've gone through today, maybe she'd be less judgmental,* Adam thought irritably. Then he caught himself. *Well how would she know when you won't tell her, you coward?*

Chapter Seven

By morning Jill had calmed down after her pity party and a thorough breaking in of her new vibrator. Her book was due to hit the bookstores in a day or so. She should be in a celebratory mood, not bawling her eyes out. Besides, she should have expected something like last night to happen. After all, it happened a great deal.

She had forgotten how important it always had been for Adam to become the director of client services. That was what he'd been striving for. All the extra hours and Saturdays had been to impress his bosses. *And how has it worked out for him? They dangle that position like a carrot in front of Adam's nose and he chases after it as if it were the Holy Grail. He does it for us, he says. Well, maybe it's really for him. She was happy with what they already possessed. Why couldn't Adam be content?*

***

Adam was able to smooth things over with Joel Fried. The delicious steak and cocktails at E. B. Green's classy restaurant helped, but, it was the fact that Adam guaranteed his ad would be on time and threw in a complimentary color spread in *House & Gardens* that really brought a smile to Fried's face.

He felt good about saving the account for the ad agency, but truly wished he could be the conquering hero in Jill's eyes. Alone in the hotel, Adam thought a great deal of how things had disintegrated between him and Jill. They hardly made love anymore—hell, they hardly spoke without jumping down each other's throats.

This was not what Adam wanted. He loved Jill and always had ever since he first saw her. He noticed her beautiful amber eyes with the gold flecks held a gleam that no makeup could improve. Those eyes were sometimes mischievous and other times dancing with laughter, but always deep enough for him to drown in. And yet, he loved her eyes most not when they glowed with enjoyment, but when they brimmed with tenderness and passion. He missed that passion.

The passion that he shared with Jill he'd never known with any other woman. No one could make him feel like Jill could. Because of Jill, he'd reached heights of pleasure he'd never thought possible. Closing his eyes he pictured her beautiful face with its delicate high cheekbones and soft, creamy, mocha skin that tasted as good as it looked. Merely touching her always sent shivers of delight through him. Her sweet kisses always left his mouth burning with fire, and sometimes he couldn't get enough of them.

Just thinking about Jill made him hard. He stroked his erection thinking about what he'd do to her when he got home.

***

When Jill got home from work, she found a box by her front door left by the mailman. She opened the door and carried the box inside. Excitement bubbled within her as she noticed the stamped return address. Ripping the box open and nearly breaking two of her nails in the process, she took out one of her books and gingerly thumbed through it. The cover was shiny and gorgeous. But the best part of it was her name in big bold letters. She had done it!

Jill immediately called Lynne and told her she was sending her a book.

"Don't you dare!"

"Why not? I want to autograph it, as well."

"I want to buy one. You could autograph it when you come to visit."

"Why spend the money when I can send you a free one?" Jill said.

"Because I want to have the pleasure of telling the cashier that this is my sister's book. Didn't I tell you that I wanted to be the first one to buy it?"

"I love you, Lynne."

"I know, and I love you, too. But hell, I'm so damn proud of you! You should send a copy of the book to Mom and Dad."

"Yeah, and I'll autograph it 'your loving daughter'— right."

They shared a laugh.

"All laughter aside, you know, Sis, if your book becomes a bestseller, they're gonna know."

"I'd rather they find out that way. If I sent them a book, they'd probably toss it in the garbage."

"Yeah, they probably would. By the way, has Adam seen it yet?"

"No. He flew straight from work yesterday to Buffalo. One of these days, it's going to be me or that job of his."

"Word to the wise, don't make it an ultimatum," Lynne advised. "Communication 101."

"I know. It just gets to me sometimes."

"Just don't let it get the better of you."

"I won't. Somebody's beeping in—"

"Answer it. I've got to go anyway. Speak to you."

"Hey, Jill," Adam said, "I'm on my way home."

"Does that mean you expect dinner?" But before he could answer, she said, "Only kidding."

"See you soon," he said.

As Adam disconnected his phone, he realized that Jill sounded happy.

***

When Adam came into the kitchen, he found Jill humming as she placed the dinner plates on the table. He'd noticed the box on the cabinet in the hall and peeked inside to find it filled with her books. They did look impressive. No wonder she was so happy.

He came up close behind her and kissed the back of her neck. She turned to look at him questioningly as he handed her a long-stemmed rose. It wasn't their anniversary, so she was at a loss for the reason.

However, she didn't care. It only added to her great mood, but it didn't stop her from teasing him. "Uh-oh! An unexpected gift. Has somebody been bad?"

"Yup. You've caught me."

Jill stopped what she was doing and turned completely around to face Adam.

"I just wanted to tell you that I'm sorry I've been working so many long hours. And that I'm very proud of you," he said, a lazy smile on his lips.

He looked like a little boy apologizing for breaking the cookie jar. But when he opened his arms and she melted into them, he felt like the loving man she'd married. A sensuous heat flowed between them. Then their lips met and all thoughts of dinner were forgotten.

In a fluid motion, Adam swept Jill off her feet and into his arms. She buried her head in the crook of his neck as he carried her upstairs and into the bedroom and put her gently on the bed. He opened his pants, pulled down his boxers and pants in one motion, and let them drop as he joined her on the bed. Quickly he hiked up her skirt and pulled her silk panties off. His fingers confirmed her readiness. She was hot and wet. A beat later, he was inside her. Jill moaned as she began to move with the rhythm of his strokes.

"God, Jill," he growled as he plunged into her. "I've missed this."

His mouth covered hers, his tongue tangling with hers. His strokes became more forceful, his hips slapping hers. As the turbulence of passion swirled around them, their movement reached a feverish pitch quickly. Jill abandoned herself to the electric sensations as she felt an orgasm approaching. It consumed her, taking her to an awesome, shuddering ecstasy.

Moments later, Adam bellowed his release then collapsed atop her, spent, as well. Jill clutched him and stroked his muscular back. She truly hoped things would be better now. Perhaps, the passion that had originally brought them together had resurfaced. Or was this the obligatory sex they had every so often, the small, doubting voice in her head asked.

Chapter Eight

Within a week, Jill's book was already at number eight on the *New York Times* bestseller list. Jill could hardly believe what had transpired. It was as if the fabric of her entire life had changed overnight from cotton to silk. True, she'd poured her heart and soul into writing her first book, but she hadn't been prepared for the results.

Call it beginner's luck, but not only had her novel gotten published in record time, it had become a bestseller. Jill was at a loss to fully comprehend her good fortune. Somehow all the pain of rejection had been avoided and an unknown novice had become an overnight sensation. Jill couldn't keep count of the times she pinched herself to make certain she wasn't dreaming.

Adam made good on his word to celebrate her publishing her book. That Saturday night he took Jill to a celebration dinner. He selected a very romantic, upscale restaurant, not too far from their house, called Limani, which meant "seaport" in Greek. The imposing stone and glass restaurant was located on Northern Blvd. in Roslyn. The décor, with Pendelikon marble columns made of the same stone as the Pantheon and large clay pots called pitharia, was inspired by the art of ancient Greece.

Dining there was more of an experience than having a meal. The restaurant had an open kitchen and served seafood from all around the world, but adhered to the traditional Mediterranean diet. Utilizing a Greek concept, fish was sold by the weight. All olive oil was imported from the Peloponnese region in Greece, the saffron came from Kozani, and the capers from the island of Santorini.

There were also two wine-tasting stations, but Adam ordered a bottle of champagne. For an appetizer, they selected mussels. Adam's entrée was a veal chop with lemon-roasted potatoes, while Jill opted for the Arctic char, a pink trout imported from the Arctic. Along with that, she had Spanakorizo, a spinach and rice dish with onion, dill, and olive oil.

Adam made a toast to Jill that nearly brought tears to her eyes. "May the sale of this book bring you everything that you desire and undoubtedly deserve. And may it be the beginning of a long career as an author."

They clinked glasses. Jill blinked away the tears filling her eyes. "That was lovely, Adam."

Adam smiled and took a healthy sip of his champagne. What she saw in his eyes sent her spirits soaring and a warm glow flowing through her.

Jill sipped her champagne and felt the bubbly slip down her throat. "This place is beautiful. How on earth did you hear about it, Adam?"

"I've eaten here before with some of my important clients."

The waiter delivered a tray of pita bread, humus and an olive oil mixture. He topped up their champagne glasses and left once more. A few minutes later, he returned with a heaping bowl of mussels.

"Try the mussels, Jill. They're unbelievable."

Jill took his advice and discovered they were delicious. Everything she'd eaten so far was excellent. It had been quite a while since they'd gone out to dinner at a fine restaurant, but the best part was spending time with Adam.

He couldn't be any more attentive. It actually made her heart sing. When he asked her to tell him about the book, she was flattered by his interest.

Now as they conversed, each time his gaze met hers, her heart turned over in response. Perhaps the bubbly had gone to her head and she was reading more into his looks then there was. However, she didn't care, because right then and there she felt wonderful. Nothing else mattered. Since she had found success as an author, perhaps her personal life would eventually transform for the better, as well. No matter what, this was her night and she would enjoy it to the fullest.

Adam pulled into the driveway at their home in Locust Valley. As he opened the passenger door for Jill their eyes met. A sensuous light passed between them, causing her to feel the familiar tingling in the pit of her stomach. Heat rippled under her skin as she recognized the flush of sexual desire. The anticipation of making love jolted her heart and made her pulse pound.

Jill had the urge to throw herself into Adam's arms. As if reading her mind, Adam closed the front door behind them and enfolded her in his arms. His mouth found hers as he backed her against the door and crushed her to him. One of his hands delved straight to her breasts, pushing the bra up over them. As he tweaked a nipple, Jill felt the sensation shoot to her clit.

When they broke for air, Jill whispered, "Oh, Adam, love me," before his lips sought hers once more.

After hastily shedding their coats, Adam lifted Jill into his arms and carried her up to their bedroom. Along the way, she buried her face against his neck and breathed in the combination of his aftershave and unique smell. Her body instinctively responded to him and she felt pleasure coursing through her body like an awakened river.

They fell back onto the bed and began to undress one another with the enough urgency to rival that of her characters. It all seemed so surreal. She felt as if she were playing a scene ripped from her novel. Script or no script, the sensations and pleasure she was feeling was real.

Jill's restless hands stroked Adam's broad, toned back and threaded through his hair as he kissed and suckled her breasts. She nibbled at his ear lobe and kissed his neck as she rubbed herself against him.

Adam's lips found Jill's once more and he took her mouth with a savage intensity. Her lips continued to burn as he planted a series of slow, shivery kisses down her body to explore her core. She felt her blood pound in her brain as she breathed in erratic gasps. Jill arched her back as Adam sucked her sensitive nub while he stroked and kneaded her pebble-hard nipples ratcheting up her pleasure.

Passion now surged throughout Jill's entire body. Her insides felt as tightly wound as the mainspring of a watch. She needed to have Adam inside her now and felt her impatience loom to explosive proportions. Taking matters into her own hands, she reached for his penis and guided it home. As it filled her, she closed her eyes and gasped with pleasure.

As their bodies began to move in harmony, they reveled in the pure pleasure of the passion flowing between them. Before long, their desire had risen to a feverish pitch. A moan of ecstasy slipped through her lips as she surrendered to the whirlpool of delight that shook her entire body.

By the time the last pleasurable sensation of her orgasm faded, Adam grabbed Jill's buttocks and pounded into her several moments before his body tensed and he reached his own climax. Seemingly spent, he collapsed on top of her.

They lay like that for several moments, and Jill couldn't help but hope that they'd reached a turning point in their marriage. Perhaps, from this moment on, things would be different. Adam would realize how much he'd missed their intimacy and spend more time at home with Jill. And this hadn't been obligatory sex.

Chapter Nine

Jill hadn't quite gotten over the shock of how well her book was doing. Her agent, Joan Wilson, couldn't be any happier and told Jill that, at this rate, she was going to be number one on the *New York Times* bestselling list.

"Major booksellers are having problems keeping the book in stock," Joan told her with undisguised happiness.

Lynne was so proud of Jill that she built up her nerve and called their parents to tell them about Jill's success. Lynne had blurted out nearly the entire news before her mother disconnected the call. Jill had to admit she wasn't as brave as her sister, but she'd wished she'd been a fly on the wall of her parents' apartment when her mother told her father about her accomplishment.

Jill was still processing all this fabulous news when her editor at the publishing house, Robin Wycoff, called to meet her for lunch at Serafina's in Manhattan the following day.

Serafina's, located on Broadway in midtown, was a trendy restaurant. As Jill emerged from her cab, Robin Wycoff was already there hovering near the bright yellow awning with the restaurant's name in bold, blue script. Next to Robin stood a tall, slim, African-American woman dressed in a smart navy suit looking like she could have graced the pages of any fashion magazine.

In an instant, Robin hugged Jill, nearly depleting all the air from her lungs before introducing Evelyn Mason, the publicist for Barnaby & Sons. As the woman spoke, Jill noted a British accent. Her high cheekbones and cultured accent made her exotic in comparison to the frumpy Robin Wycoff, who spoke with a distinct Brooklyn accent and was far from a fashionista.

However, even though Jill realized that Evelyn may have appeared classy, Robin was in a class of her own. Despite her humorous demeanor, Robin was extremely intelligent and a good editor who prodded her to do her best. After hearing about several editor horror stories, Jill had been thrilled she was paired with a wonderful editor like Robin.

Entering the restaurant's eye-popping glitzy interior, Jill's eyes were doing visual calisthenics trying to take everything in. The maître d' led them past red tablecloth-covered tables occupied by twenty- and thirty-something people, a huge black-lacquered bar with white and red polka-dot sides, then through a red archway lit with white polka-dot lights, to an intimate booth nestled between two huge, beaded mosaics picturing glamorous-looking women. On another wall was a huge stained glass window of red and yellow flames.

After Evelyn ordered a bottle of champagne to celebrate, the waiter handed them menus. Robin turned to Jill. Cheerfully she said, "This lunch is on the publisher, so eat and enjoy!"

"Can you suggest something that's good?" Jill asked.

"Look at me," Robin said, "do I look like there's something I don't like?"

The two other women chuckled goodheartedly.

"I say, experiment, Jill," Evelyn suggested. "I love going to restaurants I've never been to before and trying new dishes."

The waiter returned with the champagne and popped the cork. After pouring them each a glass, Evelyn made a toast and they clinked glasses. The two women congratulated a blushing Jill, who felt the champagne go immediately to her head. Then the waiter left, giving them time to decide what they were having.

They picked two appetizers to share: *bruschetta*, bread toasted over a wood fire with tomatoes, fresh basil, and a touch of garlic, and *sashimi di tonno*, a finely sliced sushi tuna and avocado served with a special dipping sauce.

For salads they chose the *tricolore*, which consisted of Italian radicchio, arugula, endive, shaved aged Parmesan, and pears. As for their main dishes, Evelyn opted for the *spaghetti al'aragosta*, with came with half a lobster served in a spicy tomato sauce, while both Robin and Jill ordered *jumbo shrimp al cognac.* The shrimp was sautéed in cognac sauce and served on saffron rice.

The appetizers came right out and were passed around the table. Jill realized that she had to eat something to counteract the effects of the champagne. Being nervous about this meeting, she had had only coffee earlier. That's why she felt the effects of the alcohol so quickly. She enjoyed the bruschetta, but wasn't too keen on the sushi.

As they were finishing the appetizers, the waiter brought their salads and refilled everyone's glasses before he left.

Evelyn smiled at Jill. "Your book is selling rather well. In fact, in the short time it's been out, its sales have surpassed those of several of our most popular authors."

"This is all so unbelievable to me." Jill sipped her drink.

"Hey, it's a great book," Robin added, pushing her oversized black glasses back up the bridge of her nose. "Personally, I couldn't put it down."

Evelyn laughed. "That's for certain. Robin was your biggest cheerleader. And now we're here to discuss how you can ensure sales will continue to increase."

"I'd certainly like that and will do all I can to help," Jill replied earnestly.

"That's exactly what we like hearing from our authors," Evelyn added, giving Jill another smile.

"Who wouldn't want to sell more books?" Robin asked. "More sales translate into more money in your pocket, plus a higher profit for the publishing house. It also helps raise the stakes in the negotiation for your next novel. Something every writer desires."

Her next novel? Jill had been toying with some ideas, but hadn't come up with a sustainable plot that moved her. She still hadn't gotten over the miraculous results of this one. She felt as if she was sleepwalking through all her good fortune and constantly pinched herself to make certain she was awake. When Joan had mentioned a three-book deal, it had gone right over her head. She was now on the hook not only for another book, but two.

Evelyn interrupted Jill's thoughts. "We feel your book is going to be the next blockbuster. What we'd like you to do is help stimulate sales by going on several local book signings and perhaps some type of promotional tour later to put your face out there. Getting these events booked is my job, so don't worry about that. All you have to do is show up."

She knew she should feel terrific that the publisher was betting on her book to become a number-one bestseller, but it was all so overwhelming. As she listened to Evelyn, Jill felt the color drain from her face. She didn't possess an out-going, showy-type personality. Most likely she'd freeze up in front of an audience. "Uh...I don't know...I...I've never done any public speaking before."

"There's nothing to worry about," Robin reassured her. "All you have to do is just be your pretty self and you'll do just fine."

"But...but...what would I say?"

"I'd help you with that," Evelyn replied. "We'd never just throw you before a TV camera without any preparation. We'd prepare you for all your interviews."

The waiter brought their main course. A welcome interruption. All Jill had heard was TV, which echoed in her head over and over again. And it shook her completely—down to her pumps. She'd just gotten over the idea of having to go public online with a website and blog. That was stressful enough for the type of person who often dreamed about showing up in public places naked. In a shaky voice, Jill said, "I'm not sure I'm going to be able to appear on TV—even with all the preparation in the world."

Evelyn grinned. "Don't work yourself up like that. I have a feeling you're going to be a natural."

"Whatever would give you that impression?" Jill asked in a voice wondering where she was coming from. *Unless, of course, Evelyn intended to hire an actress to play me.*

Evelyn explained. "You won't have to say much to be a success. I guess you haven't looked into the mirror lately. You're a beautiful woman, Jill, the epitome of American womanhood. You're tall, shapely, and your skin looks as smooth and soft as honey—the woman of every man's dreams, and the one every woman secretly wishes she could be."

"And don't forget a talented writer, as well," chimed in Robin.

Jill felt her face heat. They actually felt her physical attributes would help sell the book. This was something she'd never have considered. She'd never thought herself to be beautiful—or anybody's ideal. Attractive, yes, but "the epitome of American womanhood"—never. According to her mother, the maven of all things black, the epitome of American womanhood in America was blonde and blue-eyed.

Unfortunately, her mother was just as racist as the people she accused of racism. She couldn't see the good in the white race. Nor did she allow herself to trust a Caucasian. She tarred them all with the same damn hateful rhetoric. Thank goodness, Jill had the guts to follow her own conscience and heart. When she ran off with Adam, she may have gained a husband, but she lost her parents. In no uncertain words, they told her she was no longer welcome in their home or their hearts. "Maybe we'll revisit the situation if you stop sleeping with the enemy," her mother had said. *Too bad I've gotten more aid and comfort from "the enemy" than you gave me, Mama*, she thought.

"I'm sorry, Jill. I didn't mean to embarrass you like that," Evelyn said, lassoing Jill's wandering thoughts and drawing her back to the present. "Only keep in mind that there's nothing wrong in using what gifts God has given you to boost sales."

"I realize that. It's just...I never considered myself to be...beautiful."

"Well take a good, long, hard look in the mirror sometime, lady. You're a certified knockout," Robin added. "And I'm totally jealous. What I wouldn't give to have your face and figure."

Jill shook her head to protest, but to be honest, coming from Robin, who was more than a little overweight and wore thick, black glasses, Jill wasn't quite certain how much weight to give to her statement, no pun intended.

"Okay, ladies, I get the picture. Thanks for the morale boost, though."

"So you'll do it?" Evelyn asked, her face a mask of hope.

Jill nodded. "I'll do whatever I can to promote my book. Who knows, maybe it will turn out to be fun," she replied, even though her face didn't quite mirror her words.

During the rest of lunch, Evelyn gave Jill an idea of some of the promotions she had in mind. Though it scared Jill nearly out of her mind, it excited her, as well. She had no idea how this new chapter of her life was going to play out, but she was going to take the ride no matter where it took her. And there would be no looking back, she decided.

***

The first book signing was held locally at the Barnes & Noble in Manhasset. Jill hadn't expected so many people to show up to see an unknown, but they did. Evelyn had done her job to get the word out well, and it had paid off. By the end of the scheduled hour-and-a-half, Jill's hand was throbbing with what she suspected felt like the first stages of carpal tunnel syndrome. She never realized how much energy it took to sign a book, let alone close to a hundred. And it would have been more had the store not run out of books. One of the sales associates had brought Jill more water and whispered into her ear that the line snaking around the bookstore was just as long as those for some of the other prominent personalities who'd been here. That gave Jill a rush like none she'd ever had.

Jill had never been surrounded by so many adoring people, either. Sitting next to a six-foot tall cardboard replica of herself made Jill feel like a clone. A silly thought occurred to her: it was too bad the replica couldn't pitch in and sign some books, as well.

Though it was one of the most exhausting things she'd ever done, Jill had fun. She'd been quite nervous, at first, but the genuine interest and warm support of the readers chased all those negative feelings away. It made her feel...like somebody truly special. Unique.

Even more surprising, Jill discovered she rather enjoyed being the center of attention. She could easily get used to it. The wonderful dinner at Limani and the sweet lovemaking that followed afterward had renewed Jill's hope of having Adam at home more often. But, it was often like waiting for the proverbial other shoe to drop, and on the heels of hope, disappointment often came.

It was during the drive home that Jill had a most disturbing thought. Adam had continually told her that they could never live on her salary as a bank teller. What if the success of her book had the potential to change that dynamic? What if the sales from her book made her financially independent and Adam felt threatened?

She mulled that idea over. No, of course not. Adam wasn't a petty man—or was he? They were like two boats drifting apart lately, and he could feel differently now.

An involuntary chill rode down Jill's spine. She truly feared that her success might prove to be a wedge that further divided them. And the "what ifs" were going to be the death of her. Yet she couldn't avoid them.

The truth of the matter was that she and Adam had been growing apart. With all fairness, his climb up the ladder of success sowed the seeds of this divide. In his pursuit of fortune, he'd left her behind. He never wanted to be like his dad—a useless drunk who stumbled from one job to another until he drove his car into a ravine. Unfortunately, it looked like Adam had traded his fear of becoming his dad into a kind of obsession.

Adam had been correct in his assessment of her economic dependency on him; however, her publishing success could make her financially independent. Jill realized she was left with that nagging question lurking in the corner of her mind: was she still willing to make the effort to try to save her marriage? Better yet, was it at all possible now? Despite the recent great sex, was the gap between them no longer bridgeable?

Jill couldn't lie to herself. She still cared for Adam, no matter how distant he'd become. Yet, she couldn't deny the fact she needed to be desired and wanted—and loved. Sex once or twice a month was not what she considered fulfilling. And it wasn't only the sex. The intimacy was also lacking. She didn't want to be alone more often than not. And Adam never fully opened up to her. Nothing, not even writing could fill that type of loneliness.

Writing was very therapeutic for Jill. As she delved into shaping her characters, she learned a great deal about herself. Here she was empowering her women, when she was behaving like a victim. There were things she could do to try and change things in her life for the better. First off, she had to make Adam want to be with her more. If she could create characters who could seduce one another, why couldn't she do the same with Adam? All she had to do was write the scene.

Jill decided to keep their fragile sexual spark alive by seducing Adam when he came home that night. The last time she tried to do this he hadn't come home. Instead, he'd flown to Buffalo. But, tonight she felt it was safe to proceed because Adam had mentioned he'd be home the normal time for dinner and hadn't called to tell her differently.

She prepared a salad and a rice dish along with some southern fried chicken as she watched the news on the TV mounted on the kitchen wall.

Adam appeared in the kitchen. Jill picked up the remote and shut off the TV as Adam walked inside. She kissed him hello.

"Hmm, something smells good," he murmured.

"That's the fried chicken. Wash up. Everything's almost ready," she said as she went to get the salad.

Most of the talk over dinner was about her book signing. Adam appeared to be interested to hear all about it. As they were finishing, Jill put into play the scenario she'd planned in order to get Adam to follow her upstairs into their bedroom. It was a cockamamie story about needing his opinion on which blue suit she should keep.

"Okay, wait here, while I change in the bathroom. That way you'll get the full effect," she said.

Adam shrugged but smiled. "Okay, I guess."

Jill rushed into the bathroom to change into her sexy teddy. She was going to rock his world. When she emerged not more than five minutes later, she found Adam stretched out on the bed sound asleep.

Staring at her husband sleeping peacefully, his chest rising and falling gently, Jill felt tears of frustration and disappointment escaping her eyes. Then she felt a surge of tenderness as she looked at his tired, handsome face. With a sigh she got into bed and took out her new pink vibrator.

Chapter Ten

Jill had another book signing later that week. It was held at the Barnes & Noble in Carle Place. This signing proved to be just as successful. Evelyn had stopped by and was pleased enough to start arranging more signings at other locations. She informed Jill that if this trend continued, they would be looking at a second printing of the book.

Now reflecting on this, Jill realized she soon could be negotiating a bigger advance for her next contract. What scary, wonderful words. *Her next contract*? She was jumping the gun quite a bit, since she hadn't written anything concrete for her second book. Sure, she'd scribbled down several plot lines she was toying with, but she couldn't decide in which direction she wanted to go. What if she were a one-book sensation?

***

Later that day, Evelyn called to let Jill know she'd been nominated for the American Romance Writers Association award for best new romance fiction writer. The winner would be announced at the awards dinner in a few weeks. After the call ended, Jill decided it was time to start thinking about giving the bank notice.

Jill felt different after her successful book signings. It was as if she'd broken out of the cocoon in which she'd been living her entire life. She felt empowered, truly a feeling she'd never experienced before. She'd always stood in someone else's shadow, never feeling independent before. First, she was practically invisible to her parents who had put their causes before her. Then when she married Adam, it was his success that she basked in. Now for once, she was standing in the sun and casting her own shadow as she spread her wings. And it felt *damn* good!

***

On the way to work the following morning, Jill decided on the plot for her next story and hoped it would be as good as her first one. That's all she wanted—along with a more attentive husband. She was even willing to give up precious writing time if Adam would spend more time with her. That would mean more to her than all the success in the world. It was no fun not being able to have him at the various publicity functions the publisher scheduled to share in her success and happiness.

Some of the bank's patrons had already read her book and asked her to sign their copies, which they'd brought along. Overnight she'd become a minor celebrity. Even so, she nervously glanced every now and then toward the bank manager's cubicle to make certain she hadn't overstepped bank policy. She honestly didn't want to cause trouble, but deep inside she was reveling in her celebrity status.

Jill ran some errands after work and was surprised to find Adam already home by the time she got there.

"Boy, you look as if you've seen a ghost. I *do* live here you know."

He had no idea what Jill had planned the previous night. Nor had he woken while she was pleasuring herself. She suddenly felt guilty as if she was keeping a secret from him. Recovering her composure she said, "Sorry, Adam. It's that you usually work more late nights at the end of the month."

"True, but I wanted to come home and spend some time with the soon-to-be number-one *New York Times* bestselling author."

"Aren't you being a tad premature?" Jill said.

"Nah. Just clairvoyant. I see people reading your book everywhere. I'm truly proud of you, darling."

He hadn't called her that in such a long time. Jill searched Adam's blue eyes, which had become heavy with desire. "Are you?"

"Yes, I really am," he replied, reaching out for her. "Maybe I can pop into one of the signings you'll have in Manhattan."

Jill brightened and slid into Adam's arms. "I'd love that."

Though Adam's words caused Jill's heart to lift, as he covered her mouth with his, guilt clouded her mind. Perhaps, she'd been too hasty in thinking there was little hope for their marriage. But when his hands began to roam her body, all she could think about was how much she still cared for him. He had the power to make her tremble at his touch.

Adam's lips and hands quickly obliterated any lingering doubts or negative feelings she had. At the same time this demonstration of his love gave Jill renewed hope that things would be different now. Her last thought before her libido took over the control of her mind was that dinner was definitely going to be late.

Together they went upstairs to the bedroom. There was no sense of urgency in their lovemaking. Instead, it was a perfectly choreographed dance from beginning to end. Every touch and every kiss was a slow, measured movement. They undressed each other and took the time to delight in one another's body. Thus the pleasure was trebled in measure.

Afterward, Adam rested his cheek on one elbow as his eyes caressed Jill's naked body. "I've forgotten how beautiful you truly are, Jill," he said in a hoarse voice. He kissed her breast, before gently nipping at its pebbled nipple, causing her to shiver in delight.

Jill could feel the tension in her sex growing taut as she raked her restless hands through his hair and down his back. Adam lifted his head and looked deeply into Jill's eyes for a beat before he straddled her. His unmistakable look of want further heated Jill's own lustful desires. Crushing her lips with his, he clasped her hands and held them over her head. Then he slipped inside Jill and their bodies became one as they moved in an exquisite harmony known only to them.

Before long, they reached that pleasurable precipice where every stroke and every touch propelled them closer to their climaxes. The bed springs creaked as the movement of their bodies increased in speed. They kissed and stroked each other with frenzied movements. Jill felt so close, she needed to feel him deeper. She grabbed his pillow and shoved it under her bottom, which tilted her pelvis slightly. It proved to be just enough and a beat later, Jill let out a long moan of pleasure as one wave of ecstasy after another washed over her. Just as she felt her last spasm of pleasure wane, Adam climaxed and released inside her. She had but one thought. If only she could bottle this moment for all eternity.

As Adam collapsed on top of Jill, he said wryly, "Perhaps it should be a pizza night."

Her laughter filled the room.

Jill went to bed that night nearly giddy with happiness. Apparently, despite the bickering and doubts, Adam still loved her. However, it was the fact that he took pride in her success as a writer that lightened her heart.

Chapter Eleven

Adam came home from work early every night for the next several days. What pleasure it was for Jill to have dinner with him. It was reminiscent of the way things were when they were courting and they had all the time in the world to talk and make love. And now there was much she needed to talk about.

Earlier in the day her editor, Robin, had called with the good news that the publishing house had decided to print a second run. If her publicist, Evelyn Mason, had her way, *Never Leave Me* would be gracing the front window of every bookstore and the shelves of every library in America. Robin also mentioned that the publicist had a number of book signings lined up for that week and would contact Jill with the final details. Though the news was wonderful, it also left Jill with a dilemma.

Up until now, whenever she needed time to pursue her writing career, she'd been able to call in sick from her job at the bank. But, spontaneously taking several days a week off would be different. Jill didn't think the bank management would be okay with this. Though she'd decided to give notice, she'd been putting it off. Now she was out of time.

Over Adam's favorite meal of meat loaf, mashed potatoes, and corn, Jill brought the subject up. "My publicist scheduled two more book signings for this week," Jill said.

"That's good exposure. Hopefully, I'll be free for one of them."

"I agree about the publicity. It's definitely good for my writing career, but not so good for my other job."

"You *haven't* given notice to the bank, yet?" Adam sounded surprised.

"No. It's a steady income."

Adam began to laugh.

"You find that funny?" Jill's eyes narrowed, failing to see the humor in what she'd said. She merely jumped to the conclusion that Adam was belittling her job at the bank—again.

Gesturing with his fist against her head, Adam said, "Knock, knock, anybody home? You're an author now, Jill. And from the looks of it, a damn good one. Stay home and write."

"What if my next book is a flop?"

"You'll write another. Who cares? Your book is making money and I make an excellent salary. We won't miss the bank pay check."

Then it finally dawned on Jill. This was her chance to develop her new career. And if she could remain at home to write full time, then perhaps she could also finally realize her *true* dream: to start a family. Keeping her voice light, Jill said, "I guess with my being home more, I could look after a baby easily."

Adam shrugged. "I guess. Maybe sometime in the future. Let's not rush into anything."

Above all else, Jill wanted to have a child. She had been waiting on Adam wondering if he'd ever be ready. It seemed not.

***

The following Monday Jill gave her two weeks' notice to the bank. The manager, Joseph Dennings, was a trim man in his late fifties with salt and pepper hair that made him look distinguished. In the 10 years that she had known him, Jill had never heard him raise his voice. He ran the bank so well that there were fewer turnovers in personnel at his branch than any other in the area. Dennings liked Jill and offered her the chance to stay longer by offering her a leave of absence. She knew her leaving was inevitable and felt it wouldn't be fair to him or the bank staff to accept the offer, so she turned it down.

When Jill came home from work, she found Adam already home. He was in the bedroom packing an overnight bag.

"Where are you going?" Jill asked her heart sinking. "We have the American Romance Writers Association award dinner tomorrow night. You know I've been nominated for an award as the best new romance fiction author and—"

"I know. I had every intention of going, but one of the deals I'd made a while back seems to be going south. My boss feels that only I can fix it, so I have to go to Atlanta. It's not my decision, Jill. I'm truly sorry."

In that moment Jill realized that no matter what, Adam's career would always come first. And, there would always be a problem that only he, "the super adman of the world," could fix. All her newfound happiness would always be secondary. Business was business. She had kidded herself into believing things had changed. She would have to fit her life into Adam's business schedule. Did she really want to play roulette and hope that one day the ball would fall into the right pocket?

"I really am sorry, Jill," Adam said quietly, breaking into her thoughts.

"Sure. I understand." And as the stark reality struck her, Jill thought she actually did.

Chapter Twelve

Adam's overnight business trip turned into three, very long, bittersweet nights for Jill. Her winning the coveted award was thrilling, but the moment was dulled because Adam hadn't been there to share the joy with her. It would have been nice to have had him by her side sharing in her success.

Lying alone in bed, Jill did a lot of thinking. It gave her active imagination more than ample time to come up with the craziest scenarios about Adam. Of course, she knew he was on a business trip, and yet she wondered if he was really having an affair, instead. It was possible. After all, he worked long, crazy hours and traveled on the spur of a moment to one place or another—or so he claimed.

What if his lover, not content with the few stolen hours he could give her, had demanded more time, and this business trip was a concession? What if those nights that he'd come home early to Jill had made the other woman jealous? What if? What if? What if?

All those thoughts swirled around and around in Jill's head until she grabbed Adam's pillow and covered her head in a vain attempt to drown out all those crazy, unproductive thoughts. Eventually she fell asleep from sheer exhaustion.

Jill slept late. The ringing of the phone woke her. Thinking it was Adam, she fumbled, still half-asleep, for the receiver.

"Good morning!" a too perky voice sang in her ear. "Is your chimney stuffed? Is your—"

"Good Lord!" Jill hung up, uncharacteristically rude. "You should get stuffed!"

Now fully awake, Jill rose from the bed and padded into the bathroom.

***

Adam called mid-morning. "I'll be home tonight—but late. Got a lot of paperwork to deal with, so eat dinner without me."

Jill couldn't possibly miss the excitement in his voice. Even so, she wasn't prepared for what Adam said next. "The powers that be," the name he'd given to the CEO and COO, "thought I did a terrific job in Atlanta."

"That's wonderful, sweetheart."

"Yeah. That's why they're sending me to Maine."

Now Maine? Jill had already stopped listening. Just when she'd thought they had finally tethered their drifting marriage and they were growing closer, his job hijacked the tiller again. Adam would be off to Maine for an indefinite amount of time next month. *Alone again. Great title for a book—not my life*, she thought as she watched the light drizzle outside her bedroom window turn into a steady downfall.

***

Later that day, Evelyn called. "Are you sitting down, Jill? I have exciting news."

"I'm sitting now."

"Good. Your promotional tour is all set up.

"That's exciting—but scary. Who would go with me?"

"Well, for starters, I would. If you'd like, bring your hubby along for moral support."

"Evelyn, where would I be going?" Jill asked, suddenly a mixed bundle of excitement and anxiety.

Evelyn told her the itinerary she had planned.

"You sure I'm ready for all this? There will be thousands of people watching and listening."

Evelyn chuckled. "I would hope so. Listen, Jill, you have nothing to worry about. I know you'll do just fine. Just as you're doing with the book signings and receptions."

"Yes, but—"

"You'll be just as sensational on a promotional tour," Evelyn said. "Remember—you're 'the epitome of American womanhood,'" she teased waggling her eyebrows.

They laughed, and most of the tension dissipated.

When they said their goodbyes, Evelyn promised to get back to her later with all the final details. Jill would have plenty of time to take care of all the things that needed to be done before she left.

***

It would be nice to have Adam along for moral support, but following his last phone call, Jill knew it might be out of the question and decided not to even ask him. And yet, she really didn't want to go alone. Even though Evelyn would be there, it was hardly the same. She wanted Adam to be there to share in the excitement and offer moral support.

Suddenly Jill chided herself for behaving like a child. She didn't need Adam to hold her hand. It was time she took control of her life. He didn't write the book; she did. She had gone to the book signings and the awards dinner by herself. Although it was embarrassing not to have her husband's support, and she saw pity in Evelyn's eyes, she'd put on a brave front. Who held her hand there? No one. If she wanted to be a success as an author, she had to work for it. And if it called for a book tour, she had to be adult enough to do it. Besides, she had already agreed to it.

***

Adam got home late that night. He crawled into bed waking her, kissed her on her forehead and promptly fell asleep. Now wide awake, Jill stared at the wall, suddenly feeling horny. She had missed Adam and had the urge to wake him up and make love, but the desire disappeared as quickly as it had come. If Adam wasn't into it, it was just a step up from masturbation. Of course, there was the vibrator, but she really didn't feel like using it tonight. Instead, she sighed with disappointment, got out of bed, and headed for the kitchen.

Sipping a cup of herbal tea, Jill thought of the last-minute things she needed to do before she started her promo tour. She would have to pick up her business suits from the dry cleaners and do laundry. Before long, excitement had crept into the equation. Sure, Jill was a little apprehensive about going on TV, of all things, but on the other hand, this was a chance of a lifetime. She hoped and prayed she wouldn't make a fool of herself.

Chapter Thirteen

Adam was still asleep when Jill awoke at nine o'clock the following morning. That in itself was out of character for Adam. Usually, that hour would have been mid-morning for him and he'd be long gone. *Poor guy must be exhausted*, she thought. Then she remembered he still didn't know about her promotional tour. At least she'd be able to give him the exciting details over breakfast.

Freshly showered and dressed in a dark blue Armani suit, gray shirt, and maroon silk tie, Adam entered the kitchen when Jill was on her second cup of coffee, reading the newspaper. He walked over to her and kissed her cheek.

"Sorry if I woke you up last night. My flight had been delayed and it was too late to call."

Tamping down the memory of the sexual disappointment she'd felt, Jill replied, "No biggie. Glad you're home safe."

"Me, too. At least things are back on track and the client's happy. And how are things in the writing world?" Adam said, as he put a K-Cup in the Keurig and hit brew.

"Glad you brought the subject up," Jill said beaming.

"Why?" Adam took his mug of coffee to the table. "What's going on?"

"Evelyn booked a promotional tour for me. She thinks the exposure will boost the sales of my book even higher."

"Sounds like you're going to be the poster child for carpal tunnel."

"Not exactly."

"It's not more book signings?" Adam asked his eyebrows arched inquisitively.

"I'm going to be on radio and TV. Millions of people all over the world are going to see me discuss my book. I'm so nervous and—"

"Where the hell are you going?" Adam interrupted in an angry voice. Irrational fear suddenly seized him by the throat.

"So my itinerary includes booking several talk shows in New York and California. My publicist's goal is to make me a household name, like Nora Roberts."

"I don't give a crap about Nora Roberts. I'm not happy having my wife fly all over the country. Your place is at home caring for the house and me!" Adam slammed the table with his hand causing his coffee to spill onto the table. The memory of his mother returning home after she'd gone off on a bender somewhere flashed before his eyes. He reined in his galloping emotions before he blurted out things about his past he'd be ashamed of.

Dabbing at the mess with her napkin, Jill processed what he'd said, feeling as if she'd fallen into a parallel universe. It left her confused and angry. "Adam...I...I don't understand.

Why you are so against this promotional tour? I thought you *wanted* me to succeed. Writing a book is only part of an author's career. Promoting the book is just as important. People have to know it exists before they can buy it."

"When I encouraged you to get a hobby, I never expected you to be flittering around the country like some prima donna."

"*Prima donna?* I can't believe I'm hearing this. First off, my writing *is not* a hobby. It's a *career*—one that I am very committed to. It defines me —"

"Call it whatever you want. I don't care. Just make sure you're not on this so-called tour." Adam replied sharply.

"Is that an ultimatum?" Jill glared back, sudden anger lit her eyes.

"If that's what you want to make of it," he said rising from his chair. "I have to go to work."

"Don't you think we should resolve this matter before you rush off, Adam?"

"As far as I'm concerned there's nothing more to discuss. You're not going. End of story. Pun intended."

"I'm afraid that all the reservations and preparations are in place—"

"Cancel. You're sick. No problem." Adam said as he left the kitchen.

"I can't do that!" Jill called after him.

He stopped walking and turned around. His features hard, as if etched in granite. *"Can't or won't?"*

Shaking with mounting fury, Jill stood. "Both!"

Adam glared at her a moment. His blue eyes appeared cold as ice, his mouth a tight line. Breaking his stare, he grabbed his coat and walked out, slamming the door behind him. Jill heard the wine glasses in the china cabinet clatter.

She collapsed back into her chair, wondering what the hell just happened. The anger dissipated from her body just as quickly as it had come. She'd never stood up to Adam in defiance before. Too bad she felt no triumph. Instead, her eyes stung with unshed tears, while her throat felt choked with pent-up emotions.

Adam's behavior baffled her. She began to pace. Hadn't he encouraged her? Yes, he had. Then why the hell did he react in such a manner? Was he only okay with Jill having a modicum of success? Did her further potential success threaten him in some way? Why else would he be so against her going on the tour? Didn't he trust her?

There was no reason for Adam not to trust her. It had to be because of her success. She was no longer confined to the bank, but being thrust into the world. Perhaps it was a little jealousy, as well. How many times had he reminded her that he was the breadwinner—the one with the most lucrative job? Her salary as a bank teller had been insignificant and laughable. If Jill's book sales ultimately brought in more money than Adam made, their positions would definitely change. Perhaps Adam surmised this and was not taking it well.

And how was her travel any different from his business trips? Had Adam even considered he was applying a double standard here?

Truly, all this was merely speculation of her part. What Jill should be focused on was how her going on this tour would ultimately affect their marriage! Things between them had been so mercurial.

With this thought now dominant in her mind, Jill's bravado began to waiver. Her decision to stand up to Adam and follow her dream began to crumble. Perhaps it hadn't been such a great idea to challenge Adam, after all. Should she tell Evelyn something had come up and she couldn't go?

About to call Evelyn, Jill put her phone down. She sighed and breathed in deeply. If she did that, she might as well quit writing altogether. Canceling would be tantamount to shooting herself in the foot and ending her budding career. Did she honestly want to do that? Better still, could she at this point?

Two words popped into her head: hell no! Since she began writing, she truly felt alive for the first time in her life. Writing was now in her blood. No way could she stop now.

A chill rose from deep within her. But what about Adam?

***

For hours Jill thought about her dilemma and came to one conclusion: there was no easy solution. She had become an emotional train wreck—her heart pulling one way and her head tugging in another. She loved Adam, but not his obstinacy. He was definitely being unreasonable. If he truly loved her and cared about her happiness he'd understand how much this tour meant to her career. All he had to do was back off. She didn't care if he apologized or not. All he needed to do was accept her decision to go.

Jill decided to live in the moment. This was her time to shine and spread her wings as far as they would go. All this could be gone in a blink of an eye. If she worried about the future, she'd remain rooted in place. She'd try to reason with him. If she failed...she'd deal with it then.

Jill reread the itinerary Evelyn emailed to her. Her mother once said that everyone was born with a purpose and that one day Jill would find hers. Now staring at the schedule of events that had been prepared for her, Jill knew what her purpose was in life.

She was an author. She wrote books to entertain readers. She allowed them to suspend reality for a short time taking them to a different time and place. This was who she was and what she did. It defined her.

Being Adam's wife was no longer enough. She clenched her jaw to kill the sob in her throat. She was going on the promotional tour with or without Adam's blessing.

Even though she'd decided to go, she needed to talk to Lynn. Her sister usually gave her sound advice. But in this case she needed Lynne's validation.

***

Jill had to wait to call Lynn because of the time difference between New York and Arizona. When she did call, her brother-in-law, Haywood, answered. She liked him. He was so down to earth that honesty and integrity just seemed to ooze from his tall, lanky body. They traded small talk before he put Lynne on the phone.

Jill and Lynne might have been separated by 2200 miles, but their closeness hadn't changed. All Jill had to do was say a few words and her sister knew something was not right.

"What's wrong? Are things okay with you and Adam? "

"How can you tell something is wrong, Lynn?"

"By your tone, of course."

"That's nuts, you know."

"Funny you should say that, Jill. It drives my friend, Carla, crazy, too. I can't explain it. I can just tell when something is wrong."

"I need your opinion on something." Jill blurted out.

"Shoot."

"I have to go on a promotional tour to publicize my book. I will be appearing on several talk shows here in New York and California."

"That's great!"

"I know it's great and a wonderful chance to get my name out there, but..." Jill felt her eyes tearing up.

"What's wrong, Jill? Scared and nervous?"

"Yes, but that's not why I called. Adam forbade me to go."

"He *what?* I thought he was cool with your writing."

"So did I. Until this tour came up. According to him, my first priorities should be the house and him—not necessarily in that order."

"I'd laugh, if it wasn't so damn pathetic. From what you've told me, he's the one that flits around the country at the bark of his boss and hardly keeps orthodox dinner hours. You get this chance of a lifetime and he shuts you down? How selfish of him," Lynne said.

"Thank you for validating my feelings. I thought that I was the one being selfish."

"Jill, if you're really serious about making writing your career, you've got to go on the tour. Adam has to realize that."

"If he loves me, I'm hoping he will. I never wanted to have to choose between him and continuing my career."

"You shouldn't have to, Jill. Besides, wasn't it he who suggested you find a hobby, which we both know was meant to keep you busy while he was elsewhere?"

"Yup. But with men, there's always a double standard; certain rules don't apply to women."

"This is your moment, Sis. You've got to take it, because it may never come again."

"I promise to put one hundred percent into this career. Whatever talent I might possess shouldn't be squandered. I guess I just needed my actions to be validated. Thanks."

"Don't thank me. Just wow everyone else. I'm already in your pocket."

That made Jill chuckle.

"Besides, I'll be the sister of the famous author and get off on your notoriety."

This time Jill broke into laughter and Lynne joined her.

After their laughter died down, Lynne reminded Jill that her dearest friend, Carla, was a children's book writer. "With Carla writing for children and you writing erotic romance, maybe I should write, too. I could combine the two genres and write erotic romances for kids."

"Are you out of your freaking mind?" Jill asked, but Lynne was too busy laughing to reply. Realizing her sister was only kidding, she added, "Very funny."

The sisters talked about getting together before the year was out, perhaps for Christmas and said their goodbyes.

Jill knew going on the tour was the right thing to do if she wanted to help her career blossom. Calling her sister made her feel better, but it didn't alleviate the fear that by going she would cause irrevocable damage to her marriage.

***

Adam came home from work after nine. He'd called earlier and told Jill he'd be working late. For the first time in her marriage, Jill actually welcomed it. She had already come to the conclusion she'd have to broach the subject one more time. She wanted his approval and the only way to get it was for Adam to understand how important this tour was. At the time he'd called she had been emotionally drained and hadn't been in the mood to argue. Therefore, his coming home late had been a welcome reprieve.

"I'd like to discuss my tour with you, Adam." Jill brought the subject up after he had parked himself in front of the TV in the den.

"I thought I'd made my feelings concerning it quite clear this morning. There's nothing further to discuss." He depressed the power button on the remote, turning on the TV.

"Fine," Jill said and left the room, half-hoping Adam would follow her.

Adam remained in the den and Jill made a list of the last minute items she'd need to take on the trip. Still not a hundred percent certain she was doing the right thing, she would live with her decision and find a way to cope with the blowback. Or so she hoped.

Jill got into bed early and was asleep by the time Adam joined her. Nothing more had been said about the tour.

Chapter Fourteen

Adam had left for work hours before the car service pulled up in front of their large colonial house located at the end of a quiet cul-de-sac. The driver, dressed in a black suit, knocked on the double-sized wooden door. Jill opened it and he stepped inside to retrieve her luggage. Before leaving the house, Jill attached a copy of her itinerary to the refrigerator door with a magnet. At least Adam would know where she was—if he wasn't too angry to care.

The driver closed the trunk of the Lincoln Town car as Jill slid inside to find Evelyn sipping a cup of coffee from a Styrofoam cup. She looked lovely. Her coat was open to reveal a black suit accented by a very pretty, bright red-and-black silk scarf.

"Good morning, Jill," she said, handing her a Starbuck's cup of coffee.

Jill smiled. "Thank you. I seem to live on this stuff lately."

"Excited?"

"And scared."

"Don't be. You did well on our dry runs, but let's revisit some of the questions that you will be asked by Brooks Benning, the star of the *Night Owl Show*. We'll be taping later this afternoon as I told you."

Jill had slept poorly the night before. She still worried about her decision to go on the tour and her fear of making a total fool of herself. How Adam would react when she returned home weighed heavily over her like a storm cloud. After her New York interviews they would be flying directly to Los Angeles. To achieve some semblance of mental balance, she'd consoled herself that she'd set everything in motion and couldn't undo a thing to change it. What she could do was be her best and hope Adam accepted her decision to further her career. If not...

She pushed those negative thoughts away. She could ill afford to dwell on them now. Besides, she was too nervous about appearing on TV. Evelyn sensed her nervousness and tried her best to calm her.

They arrived in Manhattan and its blaring horns and kinetic activity shortly before noon and immediately checked into the Marriott Marquis hotel located on Broadway in the Times Square area. It was a crisp autumn day complete with bright sunshine, giving ample reason for people to be out and about—and they'd arrived at the height of the lunch hour. Even the hotel lobby was crowded.

Evelyn signed them in. They had adjoining rooms on the 20th floor and went upstairs and unpacked their suitcases.

Thirty minutes later, the women headed across the street to Junior's for a quick lunch. Jill had to be at the Ed Sullivan Theater at 54th Street and Broadway at three o'clock to prepare for the taping of Brooks Benning's show.

Junior's, a restaurant known for its great deli, was busy, and they had to wait at least fifteen minutes for a table. Jill watched the waiters hustling from table to table and found the noise of the restaurant comforting. It had been easy for Evelyn to tell her not to worry and that everything would be okay. However, Evelyn wasn't going to be the one seated in front of all those cameras being watched by millions of people. That thought alone nearly unhinged Jill. What would Adam think if she made an ass of herself, especially after he'd told her to cancel the tour altogether?

After they were seated and had given their orders to their waiter, Evelyn told her a little about the history of Barnaby and Sons. "The company had been started in 1888 by Sir Mallory Barnaby in London. His son Geoffrey had married an American and realized that since he spent so much time in New York, it would be simpler to just open up an office there. He did so in 1930, and a satellite office was later opened in Los Angeles."

"Are all the offices still in operation?" Jill asked as she picked at her chef salad with little appetite.

Evelyn seemed to be enjoying her Caesar salad with grilled chicken and finished chewing before answering. "Yes. You'll see the LA office when we get to California."

A woman holding the hand of her pretty little girl passed by their table. Jill imagined what it would be like to be the mother of a little girl. She wanted to have a child while she was young enough to enjoy it. Sometimes her big house felt so empty.

"What do you think, Jill?" Evelyn asked.

"About what?"

"About staying in and having dinner at the hotel tonight."

Strange to be thinking about dinner at lunch, Jill mused. "That's fine."

"Are you still with me?" Evelyn asked. "You've been awfully quiet."

"Just saving my words for Brooks."

Evelyn laughed, but Jill didn't think what she'd said was that funny.

Jill picked a little more at her salad before giving up on eating. She was too nervous.

Evelyn took care of the check and they stepped outside the restaurant and hailed a cab.

***

There was a long line of people snaking around the building in hope of snagging last minute seats for the show when the cab driver stopped at the side entrance of the theater. One of the assistants to the head of casting greeted them, but Jill was too busy wrestling with internal fears of screwing up that she didn't catch the name.

All the way to the theater she'd been a bundle of nerves, threatening to unwind. Evelyn patted her hand from time to time in an attempt to calm and reassure her. But all she kept wondering was why she had agreed to do this.

"You'll be fine. Your worries are for nothing," Evelyn reassured her.

First stop was makeup. Jill met Brooks, and found him funny and sweet. It was obvious he was trying to make her feel less nervous and, to an extent, he helped. He had brought a copy of her novel with him and asked if she'd autograph it.

It was at that moment that Jill realized she wasn't just another writer. She had started down the path of nationally acclaimed authors like Nora Roberts, Mary Higgins Clark, and Sandra Brown. Nervous, yet exhilarated, Jill discovered that it felt good.

***

The time that Jill spent on camera with Brooks Benning went by so quickly, she had little chance to feel embarrassed. In fact, Brooks made it fun and enjoyable. It was free publicity and an excellent experience for the other talk shows to follow. Hopefully, it would getter easier.

Following the taping, Jill and Evelyn took a taxi back to their hotel for dinner. And for the first time since Jill slid into the Town car that morning, she felt at ease and pleased with herself.

And Evelyn obviously enjoyed telling her, "I told you so."

Chapter Fifteen

Evelyn had made reservations at The View located at the top of the Marriott Marquis. It was a unique and unforgettable restaurant. Located high above the heart of Times Square, it revolved slowly, giving its patrons a breathtaking 360-degree view of Manhattan.

The waiter brought a bottle of champagne to their table shortly after they'd been seated and popped the cork. The sound was distinctive and numerous pairs of eyes turned in their vicinity as he carefully poured the effervescent wine into their glasses.

Evelyn raised her glass. "I'd say your performance today deserves a toast."

Jill raised her glass.

"To the next number-one best-selling author to grace the *New York Times* list," Evelyn said.

"Hopefully," Jill said, clinking Evelyn's glass before sipping the bubbly.

The waiter returned to take their orders. The champagne had an immediate effect on Jill, who hadn't eaten much that day. It loosened her taut nerves, relaxing her. She also discovered she was ravenously hungry.

Jill ordered a jumbo shrimp cocktail for an appetizer and filet mignon for her main dish. Evelyn chose the crab cakes and oven-roasted chicken breast.

While they ate, the conversation was light. Following the champagne, Evelyn ordered wine. Somehow the conversation shifted to the tourist attractions in California. Jill had never been there. The farthest west she'd been was to Arizona for Lynne's wedding, so she looked forward to seeing California.

Somehow the time rushed by and after indulging in tiramisu for dessert, they headed upstairs to their rooms. It was going to be an early taping for the Sally and Mickey Show the following morning.

They paused in front of their adjoining doors. Evelyn smiled at Jill, placing a hand on her shoulder. "You really did great today. And now that you're a seasoned guest, you'll blow the audience away tomorrow."

"Beginner's luck," Jill said, "but I hope you're right, 'cause the alternative really sucks."

Evelyn laughed. "Try to get a good night's sleep. The morning comes mighty early."

"I'm so wound up, I hope I can sleep."

"Trust me, you will. It has been a very long day and you've got to be exhausted. As for me, if I don't get out of these damn heels, I'm going to cry. Whoever invented heels definitely never wore them."

"That's for certain," Jill replied, opening her door. "Good night," she said and gave out a yawn.

Evelyn burst out laughing. "Looks like you'll be asleep as soon as your head hits the pillow. Sleep well," she said and went into her room.

Eventually, Jill fell asleep. She dreamt that she and Adam were trying to swim toward each other, but each time they got close enough to nearly touch, a giant wave crashed over them and dragged them apart. The next morning, on recalling the dream, she didn't need the likes of Freud to figure out what that dream meant.

***

Jill's defiant show of independence infuriated Adam. This anger festered, as he thought about nothing else, all the way to work that morning and remained just below the surface despite all the pressing matters he had to attend to during the day. He had been sorely tempted to call home to see if Jill had actually gone on the book tour. Perhaps the flare up in the house had been pure bravado and nothing more. Thinking it would be a sign of weakness for him to call and check, he restrained himself from doing so. When he got home it would be soon enough to discover the answer.

Adam realized it was the damn writing that had changed Jill. Her words, "My writing *is not* a hobby. It's a *career*—one that I am very committed to. It defines me," echoed in his ears in a malicious endless loop. He thought about those words to the point of dissecting them to their basic syllables to understand what exactly Jill had meant. He got the bottom line loud and clear. The writing had replaced him in her heart and soul.

It was all just simple logic. He should have known. Whenever there was a void, it becomes filled with something else. Indirectly this was his own fault. He'd left her alone way too much. And yes, he was the one who encouraged her to find something to do to fill her time—but he did not give her license to do so at his expense! It was her obsessive attitude that ultimately led to her defiant behavior. He may have given her the clay, but she sculpted the finished product.

Things had gone way too far. It might have been different if she hadn't gotten published. Becoming published and illuminated by the limelight of success definitely changed Jill. He didn't like her new attitude at all. The old Jill would never dream of disobeying his wishes. However, this new Jill was a more independent model. And with the sale of her book continuing to do so well, she'd soon be more financially independent, as well. He could not see this being a good thing. Perhaps, it would be wise for him to try and nip the entire episode in the bud—as if that was still possible. Her words repeated in his head. It's a *career*—one that I am very committed to. It defines me."

As Adam pulled up to the house, he saw Jill's car in the driveway. He exhaled in relief. Maybe he'd jumped to conclusions too quickly and misjudged Jill. Perhaps she hadn't gone on that blasted tour, or whatever it was, after all. Who did she think she was? A rock star?

It wasn't until he walked into the kitchen and turned on the light that Adam knew he hadn't misjudged his wife at all. It was all there in black and white attached to the right side of the refrigerator. Anger flared up within him as he glared at her itinerary. He snatched the phone off its base to call her. He'd set her straight.

Adam replaced the phone. Calling her in anger wasn't the way to go. After all, that's what made her more defiant in the first place. Had he not pushed her to the wall, she might not have challenged him. No, he wouldn't call now. He needed to cool down first. This situation needed more thought. Jill would have to be handled carefully.

And he had to reexamine his feelings about her. Right now, he was forcing her to choose between an exciting career and him. He had no idea, which way she'd go. To be honest, hadn't he been forced to put his career first? *Yeah, but I had no choice—she does. Besides, I'm the provider in this family. And that's what providers do.*

But, what if with Jill's new financial independence she decided to spread her wings and go solo? What if she left him? She was meeting thousands of people. What if some handsome guy came along and swept her off her feet? It was possible—of course, given her track record. Hadn't *he* swept her off her feet?

Adam covered his ears with his hands and squeezed his eyes tightly shut as if that would stop the horrible thoughts.

Reality hit him like a cold shower.

Her leaving him was the last thing he truly wanted. Jill was the only constant in his life. He'd loved Jill from the moment he first laid eyes on her. Walking into the bank where she'd worked had changed his life forever. She validated his reason for living and gave him purpose. Without her...

Adam groaned at the awful thought of Jill's ever leaving him. Not to be able to touch or kiss her... He'd miss that sensuously silky voice and her throaty laugh. The smoldering flame in her bewitching amber eyes when they made love. Her gentle touch that had the power to set his heart racing. The little sound she made when he nuzzled that tender spot on her sweet neck.

Jill was the person who completed him, making him whole. She had believed in him despite his horrendous family tree. He wasn't stupid. He knew her parents hated him and tried to force her to stop seeing him. He knew the terrible things they'd said. To them he was white trash who'd eventually take her down with him. Despite all that, Jill loved him enough to run away with him and marry him. She knew the price she'd pay for her actions would be harsh, but hadn't truly expected her parents to disown her entirely. And yet, she never blamed him once for it.

However, that was then. It was different now. Jill had changed. Had her feelings toward him changed, as well?

***

Adam didn't sleep well. He wrestled with his emotions the entire night, tossing and turning. He realized how important this writing career was to Jill. It was its unintended consequences that scared him. Her new confidence and backbone brought out the worst in him. It had made him a bully. He was becoming his father. And this terrified him the most.

As Adam stared out of the window of the train taking him to Penn Station, he thought about his love for Jill and how possessive he'd become. When had he turned into such a bully? And why couldn't he accept the success and newfound confidence that made her blossom and grow as an individual? Ironically, it would seem that these events had activated the very demons within himself that he'd tried to suppress all these years.

If he closed his eyes, he could see his father standing over his mother crouching in the corner of the kitchen, feebly trying to protect herself from the raining blows his old man was giving her. It was punishment because she'd disobeyed him and snuck into town. His mother had been beautiful at one time, attracting looks from other men. This always seemed to enrage his father. A nasty drunk and meth user, his raging tirades became more common than not.

Now as an adult, Adam wondered if it was the drugs and the booze that made him do that. Or was his father simply a monster who got off on beating his poor mother. However, she wasn't so innocent, either. Sometimes, she'd take Adam into town with her and he'd watch TV while his new "uncle" would disappear with his mother. Sometimes he had to make the TV louder to drown out the noise from the bedroom. Adam kept her secret, though. He knew if he ever told his father, he'd beat her to death.

Looking back, Adam wasn't certain if either parent had ever wanted or cared for him. If he were to guess, his parents had had a one-night stand and his mother had gotten pregnant. Why they remained together was indeed a mystery to him. He suspected they may have had some kind of masochistic–sadistic relationship. But by age fourteen, Adam had had quite enough and ran away.

Adam now feared he might possess more of his father's tainted genes than he first thought. He'd never actually analyzed his actions until now. In truth, he would never physically strike Jill, but wasn't he emotionally abusing her? He made every decision for her and molded her into a dutiful wife. Jill had allowed him to do so willingly, because she had little self-esteem. She always seemed to want to do whatever pleased him. Perhaps her parents had neglected her and Adam had become the backbone and direction that she lacked in her life. Adam cringed as he remembered how often he had belittled her job at the bank, how unsupportive he had been of her writing. They would probably be still in that destructive relationship if she hadn't gotten published. Her writing had changed everything.

And he hadn't been prepared for it. He had needed things to remain the same at home because things were so volatile at work and he found that he couldn't juggle both. The emotional quicksand was taking him under.

When Charles Aloe was removed as the director of client services, Adam expected to replace him. After all he'd done for the agency, nobody deserved the position more. Instead, he was passed over for a woman the agency hired away from a competitor. This had been the final slight. He was now ready to jump ship. Especially after he met the new director, Anna Revere, who was now his immediate boss.

Adam swore the tall, blonde woman had larger balls than he had—and brass ones at that. Her brazenness was scary, and things had to be done her way or it was the highway. It was implicit in everything she said and did. He resented and disliked her from the moment they met.

Anna Revere was also a predator. She didn't care much about rules, and that also included vows—such as in marriage. She was used to getting whatever she wanted, and Adam feared he was what she wanted. Unlike many other men, Adam didn't hide the fact he was married and wore his wedding band religiously. That apparently just proved to be a challenge to Anna.

Anna reminded Adam of his friend, Paul, also in advertising. Paul considered himself a stud. Granted, he was attractive to women, handsome in a rugged, tough-boy way, with dark good looks, but he treated women poorly. To him they were mere notches in his belt. Adam thought Anna was Paul's female equivalent. And the last thing Adam wanted was to be another notch in that woman's belt.

Despite her beauty, her overtures fell flat. Adam would never do anything to hurt Jill or their marriage. She was everything he ever desired in a woman. How he wished his new boss would understand and accept that. However, she didn't, and Adam realized he was done.

He got in touch with Jonathan Shulman, an advertising executive he'd met at a conference in Atlanta previously. Shulman worked for Simpson, Brown and Thompson, an up-and- coming ad agency in Phoenix, Arizona, and Shulman was fairly certain his firm would want a solid guy like Adam. When he'd given Adam his card, he instructed him to call him when he was ready to jump ship. Now his back pressed against the wall and a man-eater in hot pursuit, it was time to go.

Basically, this was the only choice Adam had. He could not entertain a harassment grievance. Who could he complain to, and how could he prove it? Nor could he start looking locally for a new job in the present job market. So he made the call to Shulman and did his best to avoid being alone with Anna Revere.

Chapter Sixteen

It was chilly and overcast at 8:45 the following morning when Evelyn and Jill stepped out of a cab at ABC's Lincoln Center Studios located near 67th St. and Columbus Avenue.

Jill was rushed into makeup. There she met Sally James and Mickey Dodd. Mickey was a former tennis player. Jill used to love to play tennis when she was younger. Adam hated tennis. Come to think of it, he disliked sports in general. When Adam was at home relaxing, he'd be watching the financial news channels. Since she married him, the only athletic thing she did was take long walks. When had she lost interest in things she used to enjoy doing?

The taping of the show went well. Jill walked on set to the applause from the live audience. It didn't matter if there was a lighted sign reminding them to clap. To Jill it was still a morale booster. The questions asked had been similar to those asked by Brooks Benning, and she answered them as graciously as she could. It had been easier this time knowing what to expect, proving Evelyn right. She was glad she'd taken the publicist's advice.

Jill's focus had been on the show and nothing else. She refused to allow her mind to wander and think about Adam and whether or not he was angry with her. Though she'd felt some butterflies flitting around in her stomach before she began the interview, once it had gotten underway she felt herself begin to relax a little. The highlight had been a conversation she'd had off camera with the gorgeous Sally James.

Sally remarked, "You're the prettiest novelist I've ever read."

Jill felt her face flush as she thanked Sally, trying to ignore a voice somewhere inside her head snipe, *Yeah, compared to Edgar Allan Poe.*

"I'd just love to have you autograph my copy for me."

"I would be delighted. I certainly hoped you enjoyed reading it."

"I thought it was terrific. Perhaps we can discuss it sometime."

Jill let her held breath out. "I'm so glad—and I'd like that very much."

Before long they were chatting as if they were old friends. Jill thanked both hosts for having her on their show.

When Sally hugged her goodbye, she said, "Jill, get used to being in the public's eye. I have a feeling you're going to become a *very* famous writer. We'll have you back with your next book. "

"I'd like that very much. Take care." Jill mentally whispered, *Are you listening, God?*

From the taping of the show, they had a quick lunch and then it was off to a book signing at the Barnes & Noble on Broadway.

The bookstore had done a great deal of advertising and a long line awaited Jill and Evelyn. The manager had been on the lookout for Jill and saw her enter. After introducing her to the woman in charge of publicity, he led her to the table at which she'd be signing. Awaiting her was a wall of books divided into neat stacks.

Jill paled at the books. "That's a helluva lot of books. My hand aches already," she told Evelyn as a young woman walked up to the table.

"Your bread and butter, love," Evelyn whispered into Jill's ear. "Smile and sign."

"Aye, Aye, Captain Bligh."

Evelyn caught her reference to *The Mutiny on the Bounty* and chuckled.

***

After the book signing had put a sizable dent in the store's inventory, Jill and Evelyn said goodbye to the manager and publicity coordinator and left the store. The early morning clouds had dissipated and the sun had come out, bringing its warmth. Autumn in New York was a wonderful time to sightsee, and that was exactly what they decided to do with the rest of the afternoon.

Both women were in three-inch heels and wouldn't be able to do much walking, so they took a cab back to the hotel to change into jeans and more comfortable shoes. Then they hit the street to take in the sights. It was during this impromptu stroll that Jill learned there was much more to Evelyn than she'd let on. She just hadn't imagined the half of it.

On the surface, Evelyn was a polished and charming woman. Jill was inherently curious and couldn't help but wonder if she was married and had a family. All she knew about Evelyn was what the other woman told her, which was practically nothing.

They had walked a short distance from the hotel when Jill noticed Evelyn's face had brightened like a small child's at Christmas. "What are you smiling at?" Jill asked, wondering what she might be missing.

"I love Manhattan. There's so much to do here. Just look around you. Take in the beauty of the buildings surrounding us. Some are architectural masterpieces. Like the Chrysler Building, for example. It's considered to be an example of Art Deco architecture. The tower is beautiful. And the building's gargoyles were modeled after the hood ornaments of the Plymouth, one of their major selling cars at the time."

"How do you know so much about the City, Evelyn?"

"Since I've moved to Manhattan, I visit the museums, attend concerts at the Met, and explore the streets every chance I get."

"I wish I was able to come to Manhattan more. Adam hates the city. Never wants to see a show or go dancing. For me all the culture here is wasted."

"That's a crime! Just look around you at all the marquees for the playhouses on and off Broadway. There's a show for every imaginable taste."

"Now you're digging the knife in deeper and twisting. I wish I could light a fire under Adam and get him to come."

"Sorry. Didn't mean to pour salt on a wound," Evelyn replied, giving Jill's hand a gentle squeeze.

As the women continued to stroll down Broadway, Jill's thoughts strayed to Adam. She thought he would have called by now, even if it was to chastise her for going on the tour. Her fertile imagination began to spin disaster scenarios when Evelyn interrupted her thoughts.

"Autumn in London can't compare to Manhattan. The weather is so much nicer here."

"Can I ask you a personal question, Evelyn?"

"What's on your mind?"

"How did you end up living here?"

"I divorced my husband and asked for a transfer. I wanted to start over. Having had no kids to bind me to him, I just packed my suitcase and left."

"You're a very brave woman to cross an ocean on your own like that."

"Why do you think that, Jill? When the necessity of the act becomes stronger than one's fear of committing to it, a person will do what they must."

Jill nodded her understanding and as they walked on in silence, she thought about what Evelyn had said. It was quite profound.

The wind had picked up a bit and the leaves rustled on the ground around them. Rain seemed a possibility so Evelyn suggested they head back.

"I hate to admit it, but I'm getting a little tired and could use a rest," Jill said.

"Okay. How's about we stop for some coffee on our way back to the hotel?"

"That would be great. We can rest and recharge."

"A nice way of putting it," Evelyn said as they turned around and began to head back.

The coffee shop was a welcome sight to Jill, who definitely needed to sit down. As they sipped their coffee, Evelyn asked Jill about Adam.

"It's a shame that your husband couldn't accompany you on this tour, Jill."

"He couldn't take off from work. He's a group account director at Hartford Advertising and his job is demanding."

"Does he have to travel?"

"More often than I'd like," Jill replied.

"It sounds like you don't appreciate his business trips much."

"I hate being alone."

"No kids, either, I take it," Evelyn said.

"Unfortunately, no. Hopefully, one day."

Evelyn smiled. "So what does Adam think about your writing?"

Jill felt as if she'd been hit with a sledgehammer. This was one question she did not want to answer. She was tempted to lie and make Adam sound like an ideal husband, but found she couldn't lie to Evelyn.

"The writing was okay when he was at work a thousand hours a day and it didn't interfere with him. Unfortunately, that doesn't seem to be the case lately."

"You sound angry."

"Did it come out that way?"

Evelyn nodded.

"More like disappointed, Evelyn. He should be here with me or at least have attended the awards ceremony."

"But his work is the deciding factor, right?"

"The truth is that he didn't want me to be on this tour."

Evelyn sipped her coffee. "That's not good. A husband and wife should always try to be on the same page and support one another's dreams. I hope he gives it some thought while you're away and things work out for you both." She glanced at her watch.

"What time is it?"

"Nearly five-thirty. We should head back now."

They tossed their empty cups into the garbage and left the coffee shop. Then Evelyn hailed a cab. When they got back to the hotel, they went upstairs, showered, and changed for dinner.

Chapter Seventeen

Jill and Evelyn had dinner on the eighth floor in the Lounge Restaurant. Sitting at a window seat, they had a lovely view of the city that was now lit by a myriad of bright lights against the dark, starless sky.

"I've been all over the United States, but I must confess, New York has the most beautiful skyline anywhere," Evelyn said as they ate their steak and lobster entrees.

"Honestly, I've hardly been anywhere," Jill confessed.

"That's a shame. You should travel and see this gorgeous country. At least now with your books, you'll be able to."

A sad, faraway look passed over Jill's face. She would have liked to share this adventure with Adam, but she doubted he'd ever take that much time off from work.

"Are you all right, Jill?"

She quickly flashed her a smile. "I'm fine, but I could use some more wine."

Evelyn caught their waiter's eye and held up her wine glass. A moment later, their glasses were refilled.

The conversation turned lighter with Evelyn telling Jill about London, and the wine further relaxed Jill. After their meal they strolled through the hotel and came upon a lounge where a three-piece band was playing what Adam always called "elevator music." Despite his disdain for the music, Jill actually liked it. It was great music to write to.

"That place reminds me of a small pub my ex-husband, Tony, and I used to frequent in London. It had a jukebox that only played ballads. We used to dance together so closely it took the place of foreplay."

Jill giggled. "That would make a great scene for a book."

"You have my permission to use it. You and Adam go dancing much?"

"Hardly. Adam hates to dance."

"You guys don't seem to do much of anything together. When do you have fun?" Evelyn said. Watching the expression on her face, she added almost immediately, "I'm way out of line here. Sorry."

Jill sighed. "You hit the proverbial nail on the head, Evelyn. The truth is we hardly ever do anything together anymore. I'm a workaholic widow."

"I think you may have heard something like this before, but it begs repeating. Life is too short not to try and enjoy it. Schedule dates with Adam."

"What?"

"Make it your business to set aside one day each week to go on a date with your husband. Take in a movie or go out to dinner. It doesn't matter where you go or what you do as long as you do it together."

"But what if Adam won't go?"

"Just try it. I wish I had tried harder with Tony. I might be still married to him."

Jill nodded.

They went upstairs to their rooms. Jill had to be on the set of New York Today early the following morning.

"Good night, Jill. Get some sleep. Tomorrow will be here soon enough."

"Thanks for the advice, Evelyn."

"Thank me after you try it and it works."

Jill chuckled. "Good night."

No sooner had the women closed their doors to their rooms behind them than Jill's cell began to ring. She dug in her purse and found her phone. Adam's name flashed on the screen.

Jill's face paled as she collapsed onto a bed. "Hello, Adam. Why are you calling so late? Is everything all right?"

"I didn't mean to alarm you, Jill. I just wanted to say good night."

"That's so sweet of you, Adam, but to tell the truth—I really didn't expect to hear from you."

"Why not? I miss you."

"I miss you, too, but—but you were so angry with me because I wanted to go on the tour..."

"Honestly, I did some soul-searching while you've been gone. I realize now how important this promotional tour is to you and your writing career."

"Hearing you say that makes me very happy, Adam."

"Yeah, I'm ready to make some new moves. I need to take my life in a different direction."

"Care to share?"

"It's late and I'd rather talk about it when you come home."

Even though he'd piqued her curiosity, she realized she'd have to wait to find out what he was hinting at. "All right. I'm happy to hear from you, Adam."

"Then, I'm very glad that I called. Good night, sweetheart."

"Good night. Be home soon."

***

The following morning Evelyn and Jill had a quick breakfast before they left the hotel and headed to West 66th Street where the cast of New York Today taped the show.

"Well, you look happy today," Evelyn said.

"Adam called last night. Said he missed me."

"See, perhaps things are going to be just fine. Now don't forget to make a date every week. Making quality time for each other is *very* important. Trust me," Evelyn told Jill.

"I guess you're right."

Evelyn gently cupped Jill's chin. "Girlfriend, I'm always right. You'll see. Everything's going to be just fine, because things always work out in the end."

Evelyn hoped this wasn't merely a reprieve. In her experience, men didn't gain understanding overnight. The next time Adam tried to hold Jill back might just be the last time. After all, most men fear ambitious, career-minded women. She should know. Tony had been a great deal like Adam.

The three hosts of the television show were all prominent women in the field of entertainment. Barbara Sessions had won two Tonys acting on Broadway; Lorraine O'Day had been a leading lady in Hollywood some twenty years ago before retiring to raise her family, and June Fox was a country singer with a string of hits.

Though Jill still got a bellyful of fluttering butterflies being in the limelight, she was learning to cope with them. She also was quite used to the process, from makeup to meeting the hosts and going over what would be discussed. The weird part was that when she met the three women of New York Today, they seemed in awe of her. Couple that with the fact that Evelyn had just gotten the call from Robin Wycoff that *Never Leave Me* was now number one on the *New York Times* bestselling list for fiction, Jill could now tack onto her bio the phrase, "*New York Times* bestselling author." For a nobody like herself, Jill thought this was momentous.

After the taping of the show, Evelyn and Jill had lunch at the hotel. They had to pack and head for JFK, where they would fly from later that afternoon for California. Although she missed Adam, Jill was filled with excitement. She'd never been to California.

Chapter Eighteen

On the flight to California, Jill let her mind drift while Evelyn slept. She, of all people, should know never to make rash assumptions concerning others. When she'd first met Evelyn at the lunch at Serafina's and heard her British accent, she thought her prim and proper. These assumptions led Jill to be a little uncomfortable about opening up to her. Looking back, those initial feelings were nearly laughable now.

Jill had never discussed her personal life with anyone but Lynne. She always aired her dirty laundry in private. To her, Facebook was too often used like a Laundromat and there was no way she wanted somebody in some town somewhere discussing her marital problems. Of course, social media was an essential part of an author's marketing toolkit, but Jill was careful about what she put up on the Internet for public consumption.

Evelyn turned out to be quite different from the cool persona she'd given off. She was actually fun. More important than that, she was warm and caring, and the two women grew close on the tour. Because Jill genuinely liked Evelyn, she had been uncomfortable lying to the other woman. That was why Jill had confided in Evelyn about Adam. Evelyn spoke to her as a sister. Her advice seemed sound, and Jill intended to try her suggestion about going on a weekly date with Adam. It was also a relief not to have to hide her feelings, and in this case, the truth had set her free.

One thing that Evelyn had mentioned brought a smile to Jill's face. "You know, you can call me even if we don't have some promotional gig going on, Jill. I'd like to think of you as a friend and get together for lunch or drinks some time. We can even do a show."

Jill's thoughts eventually shifted to Adam and his unexpected phone call. It was amazing how things turned on a dime. She'd started this tour dreading to go home for fear tensions with Adam would worsen. She really thought her marriage was toast after only eight years. And then his phone call had changed everything.

Jill never really doubted her love for Adam. She just didn't desire a part-time husband. His phone call came as a relief, because it gave her hope that he was willing to change. It would seem that all he had needed was a little time and separation to realize how much he missed her. Perhaps he worried what would happen if things did end between them. This meant that they might be on the same page, after all.

***

The tapings and book signings in Burbank went especially well. Jill appeared on two late night shows and two early morning programs—programs she rarely had time to watch back home because she was usually asleep during the times they aired.

From Burbank, Jill and Evelyn returned to Los Angeles, where Barnaby and Sons had another office. There she met several executives whose names she'd never be able to remember, and most of the staff. They all knew who she was, though.

At dinner, the third night they were in California, Jill relaxed in their hotel lounge with Evelyn. The day had been filled with two successful tapings and a book signing. The weather in California was delightful, and she felt tired but curiously happy.

Adam's phone calls every night gave her hope that he'd come to terms with her writing and now understood how she felt.

She replayed the first phone call over and over in her mind; something was nagging her. What had Adam meant by being "ready to make some new moves and needing to take my life in a different direction?"

"What are you thinking about?" Evelyn asked, bringing Jill back to the present.

"I guess I'm still not used to all this acclaim." Jill hadn't wanted to tell her she was thousands of miles away thinking about Adam.

"Well, you should be," Evelyn said. "This is your moment. You've achieved so much in such a short period of time."

"Thanks, Evelyn, for reminding me."

It had been a long day, so they went back to their rooms early. The following day looked like it would be another long day, since they were leaving for Chicago right after her last book signing.

***

Right before she got into bed, Jill took out her cell phone to add some new contacts and noticed that Adam had left a message. "Love and miss you. Come home safe."

Smiling, she keyed in: "Always. Loved you first."

Chapter Nineteen

Jill had hoped Adam would be home when she finally got home from her tour. In her mind's eye, she pictured herself running into his open arms and their lips meeting in a crushing kiss. Only that's not what happened at all. Instead, she returned home to an empty house.

Even though he had texted several times and called her, perhaps it was a leap of faith for her to think Adam would be there waiting for her. It would have been a nice touch, though. Leaving her suitcases by the stairs, Jill took off her coat and hung it in the hall closet before heading into the kitchen to make herself a cup of coffee. She looked around the kitchen. Obviously Adam ate dinner out every night, because there wasn't a dirty dish in the sink. *At least he missed my cooking*, she thought. *What else had he missed?*

Jill smiled. She had decided to take a positive path and try to make things better between her and Adam. She intended to strengthen her marriage and try to bring it back to how it was when they'd first fallen in love. Somehow, she and Adam would find a more permanent way to narrow the gap that had grown between them and make it back to each other.

Now that Adam appeared to be willing to compromise and accept her writing career, she hoped she could really get cracking on her next book.

The opening of the front door interrupted Jill's internal debate. A moment later, Adam appeared at the entrance to the kitchen.

"You're home early," he said.

"Yes. We gained time due to the wind current."

He nodded. "I missed you," he said moving slightly closer to her.

"You did? How much?" Jill asked moving toward him.

Adam opened his arms wide, his blue eyes burning. "About this much," he said, and Jill moved inside his open arms.

As Jill raised her head, Adam lowered his mouth to meet hers. Their lips clung to one another a beat before the heat of desire lit them both. Their mouths hungrily devoured one another until Adam lifted Jill up onto the counter. Quickly he pushed up her skirt and pulled off her pantyhose and panties. He then opened his slacks and pulled them down enough to free his straining erection and enter Jill.

Adam grunted and pumped into Jill feverishly. She scored his back with her nails and threaded her fingers through his thick golden hair. Her moans joined his grunts and together created a noisy cacophony of pleasure. Two beats later, they were both spent.

Still gasping for breath, they touched foreheads.

"Missed me a little?" Jill asked teasingly.

"Perhaps. You missed me a little, too."

They kissed tenderly and Adam scooped her up. Jill put her head on his shoulder and he carried her upstairs to their bedroom.

***

Later on, with both of them fighting a serious case of the munchies, they raided the refrigerator and found a frozen pepperoni pizza in the freezer. Jill, wearing only a long T-shirt that barely reached her knees, turned the oven on. Adam grew hard just at the sight of her. Even in a tee, she could make his pulse race.

Adam spoke. "How was the tour?"

Jill hesitated, not wanting to sabotage the lingering glow of the mind-numbing sex they'd just shared.

Adam noticed. "I did a great deal of thinking about your writing while you were gone. I realize what it means to you, and I'm not going to be a jerk about it. So, how was the tour?"

"Great, but thoroughly exhausting. I need to recharge my battery. What little energy I'd had was just depleted."

"What? You're not the Energizer Bunny?" he joked.

Jill laughed. It was more from relief than humor.

Adam laughed along with her. When the laughter died, their eyes met and held.

"I'm really glad you're home, Jill," he said, reaching across the table for her hand.

"So am I." Jill squeezed his hand. "Adam, you never did explain what you meant when you said you were ready to take your life in a different direction. You said we'd talk about it when I got home. I'm home now, sweetheart."

Adam's face became shuttered. "I know—I spoke prematurely, honey. I...I may be changing jobs but it's not something that's set in stone."

"But—"

"Please, Jill. Just be patient. I can't talk about it just now. Okay?"

Jill sighed. Would he ever fully open up to her?

God, I'm still walking the edge at work and nothing is settled with SB&T.

Adam gently kissed Jill's forehead. "It's nothing to worry your pretty head about, sweetheart. Just don't mention this to anyone. As soon as I've thought this all out, I'll let you know."

And Jill had to be content with that.

Chapter Twenty

Jill could see that Adam was making an effort to come home at a more reasonable hour. If he was going to be late, he'd call and let her know. The declaration would come with a sincere apology. She was thankful for one thing. At least, he wasn't flying off to Atlanta or wherever. This meant a great deal to her. Still, she couldn't shake the ominous feeling that all this could change in a blink of an eye. It was as if she were waiting for the other shoe to drop.

She finally got the chance to wear her new lingerie. It did knock his socks off—as well as the rest of what he was wearing. The sex that followed was hot. It also reinforced what she was learning: spicing up one's sex life with visual stimulation worked. Perhaps a skin flick would help, too.

While Jill was often thinking about sex, which was undeniably an unintended consequence of her romance writing, she was toying with the idea of having a baby. This thought was growing stronger with each passing day. She was merely waiting for the right moment to discuss it with Adam. It would be an undeniable declaration of their love that would cement their relationship and make the house truly a home.

Even though Jill was well into the fifth chapter of her new book, she'd been putting off sending Robin Wyckoff a synopsis. After receiving an email stipulating that whatever she sent would not be engraved in stone, Jill finally put together a working synopsis and sent it expecting an email back in return with Robin's comments. Instead Jill got a phone call.

"Hey there! How's my favorite author?" Robin said with her usual enthusiasm.

"Watch it! We don't want to hurt your other authors' feelings."

"They're in awe of you, girl. Trust me."

"Is this a good call or a bad call about my plot line?"

Robin laughed. "Around here, we don't use bad and your name in the same sentence."

"I'll bet. So, what's the verdict?"

Jill had been pacing as she spoke to Robin and stopped to hear the answer of this question. In fact, she held her breath.

"I like it, but..."

"But you got a zillion suggestions, right?"

"Yeah, but not a zillion, babe."

"Well, I guess that's a relief," Jill replied. "I can deal with a half-million."

"Hey, cool it. I'm the funny girl remember?"

"Sorry to step on your toes," Jill replied with laughter bubbling inside her.

"And don't you forget it," Robin said and they both laughed.

When the laughter died down, Robin grew a tad more serious. "Listen, instead of doing this via email, why don't you meet me for lunch in Manhattan tomorrow and we can discuss things face-to-face. Emails aren't immediate and are often misinterpreted. Besides, I miss you and could use a decent lunch."

Jill rolled her eyes at Robin's mention of food. "Tomorrow's good. Where and when?"

"I know just the place. It's been open forever and has a great business menu. It's called The Palm and it's on 2nd Avenue. Google it and you'll see what I mean. Will you be coming in by train?"

"Yeah. It's the easiest. I don't have to worry about parking. Hold on a sec while I get the train schedule."

Jill retrieved the train schedule to Manhattan from Locust Valley and brought it back to the phone. "The best time for me would be if I left at 10:39. That would put me in Penn Station at 11:48. The next train is much later and you'd probably starve waiting for me. So figure around noon. Is that good for you?"

"That's perfect. See you then."

While Jill was printing out a hard copy of her synopsis, she took Robin's advice and Googled "The Palm." It seemed to be a colorful place with quite a history. It was opened in 1926 by Pio Bozzi and John Ganzi and was still run today by members of the original families. The restaurant became known for its steak, even though steak hadn't been on the original menu. It became a staple because of demand. Whenever a patron asked for a steak, somebody had to run to a butcher to purchase one. *Eventually, they got tired from running back and forth*, she thought. The restaurant's walls were covered with portraits. Artists would often pay for their meals by painting portraits or caricatures of notable patrons on the wall.

Jill also checked out the business lunch menu. Robin was right. It did look good and she was looking forward to having lunch at The Palm.

***

Robin was outside the restaurant waiting for Jill when she arrived. The two women embraced and then went inside. The Palm was busy. Jill noticed there were a lot of men in suits probably having power lunches. There were women, too, but the men seemed to be more dominant. *It has to be the steak,* she mused whimsically.

The maître d' led them to a small table that had just been set up. When they were seated, Robin said, "You look wonderful, Jill."

"So do you. It's good to see you. And I'm not just buttering you up so you go easy on me."

"I intend to devour my food, not you, kiddo," Robin replied.

Teasingly Jill said, as she pretended to mop her brow, "Phew! That was close."

The waiter appeared and handed them menus. "Would you two ladies care to have anything to drink?"

Robin turned to Jill. "The Palm serves an outstanding Merlot. Shall I order that for us?"

Jill nodded her agreement and Robin said, "Two Merlots, please."

By the time the waiter returned with the wine, both women knew what they wanted to eat and ordered. They both had the mixed green salad for starters, filet mignon medallions with bordelaise sauce, a side order of cottage fries and fried onions, and New York–style cheesecake for dessert.

Robin took out her copy of the synopsis along with her comments and Jill removed her synopsis from her messenger bag. Methodically, they went through the tentative plot line together. Jill actually welcomed Robin's criticism. The editor was quite good at pointing out weak spots.

***

Adam read the email from Anna Revere twice looking for some hidden meaning. Whenever she passed him in the hall, her eyes would roam his body, no doubt mentally undressing him. When she could, she touched him, sometimes stepping so close to him he could feel the heat from her body. It was blatant harassment, but there seemed little he could do. Especially after Roy Jackson gathered the department together, prior to her arrival, and warned the men to cut her some slack for being a woman and "not to come on to her."

He looked at the email again. There was to be a mandatory lunch meeting at The Palm for Adam's account managers. The restaurant was one of the company's favorite spots to take clients because of its business lunch menu.

Now what could that woman want? She never seemed to be happy. All she ever did when she wasn't undressing the men was complain about their account numbers. At least his three account managers would be there and there was safety in numbers. Adam found this somewhat comforting.

When Adam arrived at The Palm, the maître d' escorted him to a table in the back, where he discovered only Anna seated there perusing the menu. Instinct told him to turn around and leave, but he knew he couldn't. He had a scheduled appointment to go to Phoenix to firm up his contract with SB&T first. He reassured himself that the others were just late. He thanked the maître d' and turned to Anna. "I wonder where everyone is?"

She put her drink down. "They're not coming. Sit down. You and I need to talk without your account managers' being here." Anna patted the chair next to her.

Although preferring the chair opposite her, Adam sucked in his breath and dutifully sat down beside her, his gut clenching.

"About what?"

"Let's order first. I think I see our waiter coming."

"What would you like to drink, sir?"

"A Manhattan on the rocks, please."

"And I'll have a refill, as well," Anna said, shaking the ice in her glass.

Adam had no desire to have lunch with the woman who sat next to him. He could sympathize with the fly caught in a spider web watching the arachnid approach. He really needed that drink.

As if the waiter had mental telepathy, he brought the drinks to the table in rapid time. "May I take your order now, as well?" he asked.

"I believe we're ready," Anna began. She selected medium rare steak medallions with a side of onion rings and potato wedges. Turning to Adam, she laid a hand on his thigh, rubbed it, and said, "You look like a steak man to me. Shall I order you the same?"

Adam wanted to slap her hand away. Instead he tried to shift his chair farther away from her. She just smiled and closed the gap. He was surprised she didn't order her meat rare as most man-eaters did. However, not wanting to make a bad situation worse, he looked up at the waiter and said, "I'd like my steak well done, thank you."

After the waiter left, he turned to Anna, who either seemed to be growing larger or was merely inching closer into his space. "Now tell me, what is so top secret that could not be discussed back at the office?"

"Roy informed me that your division was the top producer in the firm, yet since I've been the director of client services, your stats have decreased. This concerns me."

"Have you realized that the economy has worsened and the first item that is slashed on a company's expenditure sheet is advertising?"

Anna gave Adam a wry smile. "Good answer, Stone, but not the correct one in this case."

"As far as I'm concerned, it's the only viable one."

"Is it?" Anna challenged.

Adam did not care for the look in her eyes one bit. That look made his stomach clench again. "Of course it is!"

"I think not. And I also understand why you're denying it." Her voice grew huskier in tone.

Adam swallowed hard. "Anna, I have no idea what you're referring to. I have been actively involved in gaining new accounts and handling established accounts with kid gloves."

"But I have been a *distraction* to you. Why else would you be trying to avoid as much contact with me as possible? Because of your avoidance, I had to stoop to subterfuge to get you here just to talk."

The sexual context of her last statement was undeniable. Adam shook his head. As if fortifying himself, he took a large sip of his drink. The alcohol burned going down his throat and nearly met the bile that was rising from his stomach.

"So, I'm correct?" she purred.

"Not even close." Adam could hardly believe he said that and prepared himself for the worst.

Raising an eyebrow, Anna studied him. She was about to say something when the waiter slid salad bowls on the table. The waiter's intrusion had only been a brief reprieve. Icy fear gripped Adam's heart as he felt cornered. His apprehension about her intention toward him had been spot on, but he should have been more careful and chosen his words more wisely. So before she said anything, he tried to explain how he felt.

"Anna, you're a beautiful woman and a pleasant distraction, as all beautiful women often are. But your presence has never affected my work performance. I am here to do a job, which I've always tried to give one hundred and ten per cent. I am a firm believer in the separation of work and play. Office romances almost never work and are often detrimental. Having said that, I'd like to remind you that I am a happily married man and love my wife dearly. I hope I've made my position clear on this matter. If you find my work performance poor, I'm sorry. However, it is not due to your presence. So if you truly want to go over my accounts now, I am willing to stay and discuss them. If not I have clients to see."

Adam silently prayed as he waited for her reaction. He'd tried to rebuff her, as prudently as possible, but any rebuff is exactly what it is—a rebuff.

Instead of biting his head off and going on the attack, Anna gave Adam a Cheshire cat smile. "Let's review your accounts, shall we?"

As relieved as Adam was, he couldn't shake the feeling that Anna hadn't given up on her quest to bed him.

***

As the time passed and the lunch crowd thinned, Jill continued to discuss her tentative plot line with Robin. Jill was about to reply to a question posed to her by Robin when the people at the table directly in front of theirs got up and left. That gave Jill a clear view of the tables across the restaurant. It revealed a couple sitting extremely close together. All she could see were their backs, but there was something about the man that reminded her of Adam, aside from the blond hair. The woman continually touched him, patting his thigh or rubbing his back. Then the man turned to say something to the woman, and Jill was able to see his face.

It *was* Adam! Her stomach pitched and rolled so quickly, she nearly ejected its contents right there on the table. As sick as she felt, she couldn't wrench her eyes from the spectacle. They looked a little too cozy. They looked like *a couple*. And the way the woman touched him so knowingly, made her sick at heart.

The realization of what she was witnessing simply amazed and stunned her. She was focusing so intently on them that she'd forgotten about Robin Wycoff, who was now intently watching her.

"Are you okay, Jill?" Robin asked.

However Jill didn't hear her. Her mind, reeling with confusion and a half-dozen other emotions, simply blocked everything else out. She could not comprehend how Adam could be so tender and loving the night before and yet come here with another woman, obviously having an affair. Reality opened her eyes wider. Had all his business trips been legit? Had she been oblivious to the signs of his infidelity?

Finally Robin shook her arm hard enough to gain her attention. The tumult of emotions in Jill's head stopped swirling momentarily as she turned back to face Robin.

"Jill, sweetie, what's wrong? You look like you've seen a ghost and you're trembling."

Jill's eyes flitted back to the table where Adam sat before returning to Robin. Robin turned quickly to see what Jill was looking at. Then she asked again, "Are you all right, Jill?"

With quivering lips, Jill shook her head. Determined that Adam mustn't see her, she rose abruptly from her chair, her napkin falling off her lap to the floor. "I can't stay. I've got to go—I've got to get out of here."

Jill grabbed her purse and messenger bag, fleeing before Robin could react.

There was no use trying to stop Jill, so Robin let her go. She'd call her later to check on her. Then Robin turned once more and looked at the couple sitting at the far table. She had an awful feeling that the man sitting there with the blonde woman might be Jill's husband, Adam. And, if so, she felt sorry for Jill, because it certainly did look like he was cheating on her. God! How she hated men who cheated on their wives. Couldn't they ever be satisfied? Especially when there was a beautiful woman like Jill at home?

Chapter Twenty-One

Jill ran from the restaurant as tears began to fill her eyes. She hated crying in public and fought her emotions as best she could. The few stray tears that did escape from her eyes were swiped away quickly. Outside she hailed a passing taxicab and instructed the driver to take her to Penn Station. Hopefully she would be able to grab an earlier train out of Manhattan than the one she had planned to return on.

Why couldn't things ever work out long enough for her to enjoy them? It seemed that every time something good happened, something else had to happen to make her miserable. Why? Who had she pissed off in the heavens above to cause this? It just wasn't fair. Then she remembered someone telling her that fair was a word for children.

It also reminded Jill of a story she once heard in Sunday school when she was a little girl. According to the Sunday school teacher, God has sent an angel down to earth with a bag of joy. However, when the angel reached earth, he saw how badly the people were behaving and this made him cry. He cried so hard that some of his tears fell into the bag of joy. That was why there was sadness always mixed in with happiness. However, she was no longer a child, nor did she accept fairy tales as reality. And this pity party was over!

The blare of the cab's horn interrupted her thoughts.

Jill had to decide what to do now. There was no way she could forget or ignore what she had seen. She would have to confront Adam when he got home that night. He could then confess the truth or concoct a lie. Whichever way he chose to go, Jill wasn't certain she was prepared to handle either. Infidelity added a new dimension to their relationship problems—one that she hadn't truly considered.

Because Adam traveled often, the uneasy thought that he could easily cheat on her had occurred to Jill, but she'd brushed the thoughts aside. And now that she had been confronted with his infidelity, she hardly knew what to do. Certainly, there were options. She could divorce or choose to forgive him. All well and good. The problem was she didn't think she could rationally make such a major decision at this time. She was still having a difficult time just wrapping her mind around the implications of what she'd seen and wasn't certain how she now felt about Adam. Worse, suppose Adam loved this woman? Despite the explanation he'd given about changing jobs, suppose she was the *real* change of direction he was planning?

The taxicab driver turned around and said," Penn Station, ma'am."

So absorbed was she with working through her personal disaster, Jill hadn't even noticed they'd reached their destination. She paid the man and joined the crowd moving into the huge station. Having purchased a round-trip ticket earlier, she proceeded to the huge board to see when the next train on the Oyster Bay line would be departing. Her tear stained, blurry eyes read: 3:27 PM. That would put her into Locust Valley at 4:36 PM.

She purchased a coffee and sat down to wait. For the first time since she had run out of The Palm, she thought of Robin Wyckoff and what the woman must've thought of her behavior. Her actions had to have seemed bizarre at best. She would have to call Robin and apologize. But at the moment that was the least of her problems.

There was another approach Jill could take with Adam. It was the easiest and, of course, what she'd always done best—avoid dealing with problems. Though it was the cowardly way, by doing so, she could delay the lies and deceit for now until she was ready to deal with them. Jill needed time to sort out her feelings first. Her sister, Lynne, was always a good listener, as well as good counsel. She needed both of Lynne's skills now.

She suddenly missed Lynne and her niece, Chloe, desperately. Now, more than ever, it was time to go to Phoenix.

When Jill got home, she took off her coat, dropped her purse on the kitchen table and powered up her laptop. While she waited, she made herself a cup of coffee.

Now that she had chosen a course of action, she felt more in control and began scouring the schedules of airlines that flew to Arizona. Leaving the same day, she knew would reduce her choices, but she still wouldn't take anything but a direct flight. She was in no mood to add a stop to a five-and-a-half hour flight.

The only viable flight was on JetBlue, which left JFK airport at 8:28 PM and would arrive at 10:47 PM in Phoenix. It would take five hours and nineteen minutes, which she could live with. Glancing up at the time, Jill realized it was nearly 5:30 PM. Traffic was going to be a bitch going westbound on any major highway at this hour so she needed to give herself enough time to get to the airport and go through security. That meant she had to pack as quickly as possible and get on the road.

Putting her coffee cup into the sink, she rushed upstairs to change and pack. Noticing the overcast sky as she drove home from the train station, Jill hoped it didn't rain. Inclement weather only served to snarl traffic and tack on travel time. And she was cutting it close, as it was.

Late November in Phoenix, the temperature was usually in the low 60s, so she packed accordingly, taking enough clothing for at least a week. She'd purchased a one-way ticket, leaving her options to return home open.

Descending the steps, luggage in hand, Jill tried to think of anything she might have overlooked. She placed her laptop into its padded sleeve and zipped it. Shouldering it, she took one last look around. Satisfied she had everything she needed, Jill got into her coat, scooped up her keys, grabbed her purse, and closed the door behind her.

It had started to rain. Jill sprinted to the car, opened the trunk, and put the suitcase inside. Then she got in the car, placing her laptop and purse on the passenger seat. She started the engine and pulled out of the driveway. By the time she reached the end of her block, the rain was pelting her windshield.

The roads on the north shore of Long Island were narrow, dark, and sometimes serpentine with heavy foliage on both sides. Jill would have loved to put her brights on to see better, but they would blind anyone approaching from the opposite direction, not to mention the car in front of her. She'd been driving a short time when she'd remembered that she hadn't called Lynne to tell her that she was coming.

Technology is a wonderful thing and Jill embraced it. The Bluetooth in her car enabled her to make phone calls and adhere to the "hands-free" cellular phone law passed in New York. She glanced down a fraction of a second to engage the call button on her steering wheel. As the mechanical voice said, "Say a name or call a number," she looked up and out the windshield as bright, reflective, yellow eyes were caught in the beam of her headlights. She turned the wheel sharply to the right to avoid hitting the animal, but skidded on a slick, wet patch in the road. A second later, she was airborne as the car's tires left the road and hydroplaned over the embankment.

Seeing the blackness of the night swallowing her up as she became airborne, Jill knew these were her last moments on earth. She never expected to spend them this way. Ironically, she had always envisioned those final minutes to be with Adam, but because of him, she was going to crash and die alone.

The car hit the ground with such force that it bounced and rolled. Jill's head slammed against the door on the first impact, and she was unconscious by the time the air bags engaged and the Sonata came to a complete stop on its roof.

Chapter Twenty-Two

Robin Wycoff left the restaurant shortly after Jill and went directly back to her office. She was troubled by Jill's abrupt departure after seeing the man with the woman at the other table and wanted to make certain Jill got home safely. Jill had become more to her than just an edited manuscript. She was genuine—not egotistical as some of their other top-selling authors were—and a delight to work with.

Taking out her cell phone, Robin scrolled down her list of contacts until she came to Jill Stone. Then she hit call. It rang and rang until she heard Jill's personal message. Because it was Jill's personal phone and not her home phone, Robin felt it was safe enough to leave a message.

"Hey Jill, it's Robin. You ran out of The Palm as if being chased by a hungry bear. Just checking to make sure you outran the bear and are okay. Please call me back and let me know you're all right."

The stack of manuscripts waiting on her desk to be edited called to Robin, and she was forced to put her worries about Jill aside.

****

Adam got back to the office still seething from the horrid lunch he had been forced to endure with Anna Revere. He wasn't certain how much longer he could endure her advances. Thank God he was going out to Phoenix in a couple days to meet with the SB&T management team to finalize his move. He was done here. Let Anna Revere come on to a guy who desired her.

He grabbed his leather Louis Vuitton messenger bag, a birthday gift from Jill, and went to see his last client of the day. Afterward, he'd head straight home. After the rotten day he'd had, he couldn't wait to see Jill. He smiled. *Yeah, things with her had become so much better, lately.*

***

"What the hell!" The man in the car behind Jill's cried out as he saw her car go over the side. He immediately pulled over and called 911 to report the accident. Rushing to the spot, he looked down and saw the car at the bottom resting on its roof, its tires still spinning. It looked like a giant turtle stuck on its back.

He was getting soaked, so he got back into his car and waited for help to arrive. The rain was coming down harder again, and he knew it would make the rescue more difficult—if the driver was even still alive.

Sirens could be heard several minutes later. He got out of his car to flag them down. A police car pulled off the road, stopping not more than a yard away from him. It was followed by a fire rescue truck. The man told the officer what he'd seen and took him to the spot where the car had left the road. The policeman looked down and uttered one word. "Jesus!"

The firemen joined the two men peering over the edge. Despite the inclement weather conditions, the firemen had been trained for emergencies like this. Two were lowered one at a time by rope to the bottom of the ravine. They approached the car. Noting there was one occupant inside, they tried the doors, but they were too badly bashed in to open. The windshield was buckled and shattered, but still was attached. They radioed up for the equipment they'd need, and then the firemen went to work as quickly as humanly possible.

***

Adam got home around 6:30, surprised not to find Jill's car in the driveway. He got out of his car and went inside. After wiping his feet and taking off his coat, he dropped his messenger bag by the hall table and went into the kitchen to see if she'd left a note. As far as he knew, all she had planned for the day was a business lunch with her editor,

Robin Wycoff. Seeing no note, he began to worry. This was so unlike Jill—totally out of character.

He hit the speed dial for Jill's cell phone. All he got was her voicemail. He didn't like this one bit as he went upstairs to get out of his suit. Walking into their bedroom, the first thing Adam noticed was Jill's blue suit lying on the bed. She'd been home and changed. So where had she gone? He undressed and put on jeans and a sweatshirt before going to the bathroom.

While there, he glanced at the counter and noticed that Jill's hairbrush was gone. So was her makeup case. Her toothbrush was no longer in the rack next to his. The spot where she kept her birth control pills was empty, as well. Wherever she went, she intended to remain at least overnight.

Adam checked further and discovered that one of their suitcases was missing. Gone, as well, was Jill's laptop. A bad feeling began to fester in his gut and started to spread through him. The only place he could see Jill flying off to on the spur of the moment was Arizona. Had something bad happened to Lynne, Haywood, or Chloe?

He rushed over to the landline and hit the speed number for Lynne. There was no answer at home. Then he remembered the time difference and called her cell. He still got no answer, but this time left a message for her to call him. He'd follow Jill out there if something had happened.

"Jill, where the hell are you?" he said aloud to the empty house.

Not knowing where she had gone was nerve-wracking. Adam didn't know what to do until he heard from Lynne. He made himself a cup of coffee and sat down. As he sipped the hot beverage, it suddenly occurred to him that Jill had most likely felt the same way he now did while waiting for him to come home all those late nights. Not knowing where your loved one was had to be one of the most awful feelings. It had never occurred to him until now.

What was that saying: something about walking a mile in my shoes? And when Jill had complained, what had he told her? He'd insisted she fill those empty hours with a hobby. He shook his head with self-disgust. *What the hell was I thinking?*

The doorbell chimes rang interrupting his thoughts. He put the cup down and went to answer the door. His heart immediately dropped to his knees when he opened it to find two policemen.

A lump caught in Adam's throat and he swallowed hard to dislodge it. "Can I help you, officers?"

"Are you Adam Stone?" The taller of the two policemen with the name tag, Tilles, asked.

"Yes."

"May we step inside a moment and out of the rain?" asked Briggs, the other policeman.

Adam opened the door allowing the men to pass. He was about to ask what was wrong when Officer Tilles spoke. "Do you own a silver Sonata, Mr. Stone?"

"Yes. My wife, Jill drives it—did something happen to Jill?"

"She had an acc—"

"Is she all right?"

Officer Tilles tried again. "Mr. Stone, if you don't let me speak, I can't tell you what happened."

Adam nodded, but clenched his fists by his side.

"She's on route to Glen Cove Hospital. We'll escort you there."

"Is she all right?"

"We have no information on that. She was alive when we left. We came as soon as we ID'd you as the owner of the car," Briggs replied.

"Where did the accident happen?"

Briggs continued. "Only a few miles from here. Her car went off the road into a ravine. As soon as it is recovered, it will be towed to the police pound where it will be inspected for any evidence of malfunction. All recoverable personal effects will be removed and given to you."

The term personal effects sounded so cold and final to Adam, it caused him to shiver involuntarily, but before the police officer could say another word, he grabbed a coat, his wallet and keys. Then remembering his cell phone he went back to the kitchen to retrieve it and turned off the house light.

As Adam drove to the hospital, he tried to tamp down his fear that Jill was going to die. He remembered the time when the police had come to tell his mother that his father had driven his car into a tree. She had burst out laughing. The cops had looked at her as if she had lost her mind. In a way she had. His mother had served as his father's punching bag for years—when she'd been home. Many a night she was elsewhere, most likely drinking, doing drugs, and selling her body to pay for the drugs. Who knew what went on in her scrambled mind?

Adam had often wondered if his parents had ever even loved one another. However, he loved Jill and would do anything, including bargaining with the devil, to make her all right. It was because of Jill he rose each morning to meet the day. If she didn't pull through this, he didn't know what he might do.

The police car parked by the emergency entrance to the hospital and the officers waited until Adam parked his car. Officer Briggs got out. "I hope your wife will be all right. Good luck."

Adam thanked the officer and went inside. He found the triage window and identified himself. All he was told was that Jill had been rushed into surgery and was still there. He would be notified when she was out of surgery and in recovery. No matter what he asked, he felt as if he were talking to a robot programmed to give only certain answers.

The waiting room was nearly full with other people either waiting to hear word about their loved ones, or waiting to be called to see the doctor themselves. Looking around him, Adam noticed sickness and pain did not discriminate between the sorry-looking people sitting on the hard plastic chairs. It appeared that the only thing that got you in to see the doctor faster was the severity of your illness. An Asian man sat in obvious pain holding his arm, while a Latino father cradled a crying, red-faced baby in his arms. A blond five- or six-year-old child had his head in his mother's lap as she gently stroked his hair.

If he didn't hear news about Jill soon, Adam felt he'd surely go mad. Not knowing whether or not she would be all right frightened him more than anything. He seemed to be in the dark about everything. Lynne hadn't called him back, either. He had no idea what was happening in Phoenix—if anything, because he wasn't even certain that was where Jill was heading.

Adam needed something to do with his hands, so he went over to the coffee machine and purchased a cup. He sat down in the back of the room and slowly sipped it. A hodgepodge of thoughts swirled around inside his head like portents—unfortunately, all bad. His cell phone rang and he nearly spilled the coffee. He put the cup down and fumbled for his phone.

It was Lynne—finally. "Hey, what's going on?"

"That's why I called you, Lynne. When I came home from work, Jill was gone, suitcase and all, and I thought she was going to you." He started to choke up. "But she had an accident—"

"Adam, where are you?"

"The emergency waiting room at Glen Cove Hospital."

"How is Jill?" Lynne asked in a voice filled with apprehension.

"I don't know a damn thing, and I'm worried."

"So you haven't spoken to the doctor yet?"

"No.

"Adam, why did you think Jill was coming to visit me—especially if she hadn't told you? Had you two had a fight?"

"No fight. I thought something had happened to one of you guys."

"Jill would have called and told me her flight details if she was heading to Phoenix. Something's not right here. Are you sure things are good between you two?"

"They couldn't be better. Ever since she returned from her book promotion tour we couldn't have been any happier. I swear it!" Adam insisted as he ran a hand through his thick hair.

Lynne sighed. "Look, I'll fly out there as soon as I can. As to where Jill had been going, I'm sure there's a simple explanation. Hang on, Adam. I'll see you soon."

***

As Adam waited to hear news about Jill's condition, time seemed to have slowed, taking two minutes backward for every minute forward. Over and over again, he tried to understand what would have been so important to make Jill leave like that. He'd told Lynne the absolute truth. His relationship with Jill had gotten better. They had smoothed out the rough edges concerning her writing and were growing closer once more. The only troublesome spot was his job, but he hadn't really gone into any detail about that with Jill. He hadn't even told her that he was on the point of finalizing a move to the SB&T Agency in Phoenix. Even if she found out about that, surely she would have been okay with moving closer to Lynne.

So what the hell happened to make Jill take off like that without leaving a note? That woman left a note for everything.

Adam heard his name called and rushed over to the triage window, hoping it was word about Jill.

"I'm Adam Stone. How's my wife?"

"Your wife is still in surgery, but a policeman dropped this off for you."

Adam was handed Jill's laptop case and a plastic bag. He took the items back to his chair and sat down. He had truly hoped to hear something—anything. Inside the plastic bag, he found Jill's purse, keys, sunglasses, GPS, and registration and insurance cards from the car. He was truly surprised to see the laptop in one piece. A folded paper stuck out of the outside pocket of the case. He pulled it out and opened it to discover it was a printout of her airline ticket. She had been scheduled to fly out of JFK to Phoenix, as he had suspected. Perhaps she had meant to call Lynne from the car, but the accident occurred before she had the chance. But that still didn't explain *why* she was going to Phoenix in the first place—especially without telling *him*.

He had an idea. Perhaps Jill had made or received a phone call that could explain her actions. Opening her purse, he found her cell phone. The first thing he noticed was an unanswered voicemail.

Adam listened to the message. It had been from Robin Wycoff, her editor. "Hey Jill, it's Robin. You ran out of The Palm as if being chased by a bear. Just checking to make sure you outran the bear and are okay. Please call me back and let me know that you're all right."

Adam felt as if he'd been pierced by a knife. Jill had been at The Palm. Of all the restaurants in Manhattan, she had to end up at The Palm and see him with Anna Revere. That skeevy bitch had been all over him. Adam didn't have to be a genius to figure out what had gone on in Jill's mind as she watched him and Anna together. What it must have looked like to her. *Jeeze.*

Obviously, she ran out of the restaurant thinking that he'd been cheating on her. Of course, she'd think that. Jill had no idea what kind woman Anna was or that she'd been sexually harassing him since she'd become his boss. He had kept all that from her. Now he realized, a bit too late, that he should have confided in her. Looking at the big picture, no wonder she was leaving him. And it was because of his own macho stupidity.

How was he ever going to convince Jill of the truth? She probably had no intention of even listening to him. He ran his hand through his hair and sighed. He had no idea how if ever he could fix this. His head began to throb as the cold knot in his stomach twisted tighter.

An awful thought made him feel even sicker. He had indirectly caused Jill's accident. He may not have been there, but it was his fault just the same. She had to have been upset over his *infidelity*. On a normal night, traveling the roads around their place was difficult. Add inclement weather, and they were damn dangerous.

Adam dropped his face into his hands. He had made a total mess of everything. And Jill's life hung in the balance because of it.

Chapter Twenty-Three

Adam was miserable. He wanted to put his fist through the waiting room wall. He felt pressurized, ready to explode. And yet, he was powerless, unable to do anything to influence the outcome. He wore his frustration like a shroud. Tears of anger and angst filled his already red-raw eyes. He was the one common denominator, the catalyst that set the entire disaster into motion. If Jill didn't survive, he would never forgive himself. His self-loathing didn't allow for any slack. He deserved all retribution. This was all on him.

And if Jill survived, he doubted she'd come home to him. He could not blame her, because this self-loathing that he felt was so real he could taste it. He hated to admit it, but Jill's parents had been so right about him. White trash only begets white trash. And that described him perfectly.

The moral compass that guided his parents had not included religion amongst everything else. He could not remember the last time he'd been in any of God's houses. Being a drunkard and a bully, his father had had no time for piety. Had he worshiped a deity, it would have been Darwin, for his father believed only in the survival of the fittest. As for his mother, the only nutriment in her milk was alcohol or cocaine.

Yet here he was, leaning against the back of the chair in front of him, praying with all his heart to a God with whom he had no familiarity, begging Him to save Jill's life and make her whole again. That's all that mattered now. If he lost her love... he could live with that as his penance. But he couldn't live if she perished. Nor did he want to. If by some miracle his marriage was saved, he swore he would do things differently. What good was having money and a nice house if all that mattered to him could be taken away in the blink of an eye? Life and love were too precious to squander.

He looked up to see a doctor in bloodstained scrubs approach and got to his feet. His heart lurched.

"Mr. Stone?"

As Adam nodded, fear tightly gripped his vocal cords and though the room was warm and windowless, a cold sweat broke out along his back.

"I'm Dr. Berger. Your wife is one lucky woman. Personally, I'm amazed she survived. The concussion and punctured lung gave us some concern, as well as the internal bleeding, which was caused by damage to the spleen; but we've got the bleeding under control. She has several badly bruised ribs, and the punctured lung, collapsed. Her left arm sustained two breaks. Add to that lacerations and general bruising, and you've got the entire picture."

Bile rose in Adam's throat and he swayed slightly. Dr. Berger steadied him and sat him down.

"Mr. Stone, the prognosis is good. I'm not certain how long she'll have to remain here, but your wife is going to make a full recovery. She's in post op and will be taken to the ICU in about twenty minutes. You can see her then."

As relief washed over Adam, he shook the doctor's hand and thanked him. "You saved my wife's life. I thank you with all my heart."

The doctor smiled. "That's what we try to do, Mr. Stone. We put people back together again."

The tears that had been welling in Adam's eyes spilled over his cheeks as he watched the doctor walk away. Adam looked up toward the ceiling. "I owe you one." Wiping his eyes, he thought about his next hurdle—saving his marriage.

***

As Adam walked into the ICU, he heard the humming and beeping of the monitors attached to Jill. He could hardly recognize her. The parts of her face not bandaged were covered in reddish-purple bruises reminding him of grapes. Her head was swathed in bandages and her left arm immobilized in a sling. Though she was covered by a sheet, it looked like her torso had been wrapped in bandages, as well.

It was way too late to call Lynne, so he left a text message on her cell phone telling her that Jill was going to be all right. He reread those precious words before he sent them. They were the most beautiful words he'd ever typed.

Adam wanted to rush over to Jill and plant kisses all over her bruised face. Of course, he feared touching and hurting her, but not as much as he feared her reaction on seeing him. What if she opened her eyes and recoiled at the sight of him? So instead, he pulled the chair over to the side of her bed and watched her sleep. The slow rising and falling of her chest reassured him. Despite what the doctor had said, he feared something would go wrong and he'd lose her, so he laid his head on the bed next to her and listened carefully to the rhythmic hum of the monitor before he fell asleep.

Later, when Adam awoke, he looked at his sleeping wife and fresh tears filled his eyes. You truly never know how much things mean to you until you nearly lose them. There was so much he wanted to tell Jill. So much she needed to know. Things that he should've told her and didn't. And now it might be too late to save their marriage. Adam began to sob uncontrollably.

"A...dam..."

Adam looked up. Jill's eyes were open.

"Oh, Jill, baby, I'm so sorry," he said, swiping at his tears. Then his words tumbled out like water rushing through a breached dam. "This is all my fault. I can't blame you if you don't love me anymore, but no matter what you think, I never cheated on you. The woman you saw me with in the restaurant is Anna Revere, my boss. Had I told you about what's been going on with my job instead of keeping it inside, you'd understand what I've been going through at work. Everything went to crap after the company was sold. The new management let many people go—people that had been there for years. You can't imagine how many times I would go to work wondering if that day was my turn to receive a pink slip. Less staff meant more work and later hours. I should've told you. It would have explained all the trips and late nights."

Adam reached for a tissue to wipe his face. He clasped Jill's uninjured hand gently.

"I was able to deal with the stress and extended workdays, but then management hired Anna Revere, who made my life a living hell. She came on to me, but I feared that if I took out a sexual harassment charge against her, I would lose my job. I knew we would be able to survive until I got another job, but it was against everything I believed in to be dependent on you.

"I beg you to forgive me..." Adam was now sobbing again and couldn't speak any longer.

Tears flowed down Jill's face. One eye, being so badly bruised, was half shut. Adam grabbed another tissue and gently dabbed at her tears.

"Thirsty..."

Adam gently spooned some ice chips between her battered lips. Looking directly into Jill's eyes, he asked, "Can you forgive me for being so damn stupid?"

She replied weakly. "When I saw you with that woman, I thought you were cheating."

"I love you. I'd never cheat."

"I ran away. I couldn't face you."

He sighed audibly and gently laid his face on the pillow next to hers. "I love you. You're my entire life. Because of you, I can face each new day. If you don't want me anymore, I don't know what I would do. You know that, don't you?"

"We were both right, as well as wrong. Mistakes were made. I couldn't make decisions and you made them for me. I grew a backbone and you feared the result."

"Now what?" Adam asked, though he thought he knew the answer.

"We go forward. I have loved you way too long to try and break the habit now."

Adam kissed her good hand. His tears filled his eyes again. When he looked up, Jill was crying, as well.

"I called Lynne. She's flying out sometime today."

The nurse came in to check on Jill. "She's very lucky," she said as she began to check Jill's vitals.

"I know, and so am I," Adam replied and watched the nurse leave.

"I have your laptop if you'd like to write while you're recovering. It survived the crash."

Jill tried to laugh, but couldn't. "How will I type?"

"What about dictating to me in a few days when you feel up to it?" Adam suggested.

"You have work."

"I'm calling in sick and won't go back until you're better."

"Really?"

"Absofunkinlutely," Adam replied. "I'm staying right here with you."

"Adam..."

He raised his head and met her gaze. Their eyes locked. He tried to read what hers were saying. "The accident wasn't your fault. I swerved to avoid a deer."

"You wouldn't have been there if I hadn't kept secrets from you."

She nodded. "We both did dumb things."

Adam smiled. "Does that mean you're not going to kick me out?"

"Nope. I'm a sucker for blond, blue-eyed men. And if that Anna dares to go near you again, I'll kick her skinny butt to the moon."

"Good. Because there's a great deal you and I have to discuss about our future."

"Such as—"

Lynne came rushing in like a tornado. "You look like crap! How do you feel?"

Adam turned to face his sister-in-law. "You always make such a grand entrance."

"Yeah, don't I? As soon as I learned you'd be okay, I decided you both should spend Christmas with us in Arizona."

"We might be there sooner," Adam said.

Both women looked at him, a mirror of surprise.

"I may begin work at an agency in Phoenix before then. I'm going out there in a couple days to firm up my contract. I'm so sorry I kept all this from you, Jill."

"Oh, Adam, I should kick your butt, but I forgive you. I'd love to live in Phoenix."

"Now you have a reason to get better. Phoenix will be a great place to raise the kids, too," Adam murmured.

"Whose kids?" Lynne asked.

"Our kids," Adam replied. "Jill and I have some unfinished business to take care of."

"I see. Oh, by the way, Sis, while you're lying around in bed, your book is now number one on several bestseller lists. You'd better get cranking on your next one."

Read on for a sneak peak at

Read on for a sneak peak at

NEVER IS NOT FOREVER

by Candy Caine
Now Available

Chapter One

Claudia Brown was horny. The combination of good wine, male pheromones and aftershave—not to mention the fact she couldn't remember the last time she'd even had sex—was all it took. Okay, Darnell was hot with a decent body that towered well over her 5'11" frame and that was a plus. Personally, she hated talking to the bald spots on little men. And the fact that she didn't mind looking at his handsome face with those soft molasses-colored eyes of his didn't hurt, either.

By the time Darnell drove her home, she was primed and ready to jump his bones. Judging by the smoldering kiss he gave her at the apartment door, she could tell he was ripe for conquest and went in for the kill.

"Would you like to come inside, Darnell, for a nightcap?"

His answer was a wide gotcha-grin revealing a set of nearly perfect white teeth making her stop and wonder exactly who the *real* shark was in her little scenario.

"Nice crib," he said as his gaze traveled around the living room taking in the comfortable chairs and a sofa in soft earth-tones.

Watching him; gauging his reaction, Claudia took off her coat. "Thanks. Make yourself at home." Figuring some nice mood music would complement things, she went over to the stereo and selected an Alicia Keys CD and popped it in the player. Then she headed toward the kitchen for the bottle of wine she had chilling in the refrigerator.

When she returned holding two glasses, Darnell had taken her up on the suggestion and had removed his sports jacket. She couldn't help but notice how his shirt hugged his wide, hard chest. They sat facing each other on the sofa sipping their wine. Then Darnell put his glass down on the coffee table and reached for hers, placing it on the table beside his. "Let's dance, Claudia," he said, stretching out his hand.

Claudia took his hand. They rose from the sofa together and she melted into his arms. He wrapped his arms around her ass and pushed her bottom firmly into his cock bulge. Her immediate response was to rub herself against him. For her, it was a win-win situation and she definitely enjoyed her half of the results.

As they slow-danced in place to the mellow vocal strains of Alicia, Claudia ran her restless hands up and down his hard, muscled back. His response was to sweep her long black hair to the side enabling him to nuzzle her neck a few moments before seeking out her lips. The man was definitely a good kisser. He outlined her waiting lips with the tip of his tongue before covering her mouth with a heart-stopping kiss that nearly sucked all the breath out of her. When his lips were finished with Claudia's mouth, it felt on fire and that wasn't the only place within her heating up.

Claudia repositioned her legs in order to rub her entire pussy on his now straining cock bulge. So she'd be able to feel his hot flesh, she tugged the back of his shirt out from his slacks. Darnell slipped his hands under her sweater seeking out her breasts which were already aching for his touch. He pushed the lacy cups aside and began to caress them. Wanting him to have total access to them, Claudia moved back away and pulled the sweater over her head and unclasped her bra, tossing both items onto the sofa.

Darnell smiled and said, "Beautiful, baby girl," before he closed his large hand over her left breast and began to suckle at her right one.

Claudia moaned and raked his back with her nails. He was driving her slowly crazy as he first gently lathered her nipple with his tongue before nipping at it. Her juices, which had been simmering within her, were now pooling in her panties and her blood was beginning to boil. She grabbed the zipper on his slacks and slipped it down, freeing his beautiful, hard cock. She covered its head with her hand and stroked it down to his balls and then back up again. Darnell made a growling sound deep in his throat.

His hands were now buried under her skirt, slowly feeling their way up her long, coffee au lait legs, his fingers skimming the bottom of her panties. Claudia made things easier for him by removing her skirt and slipping out of her panties. His eyes were now riveted to her naked body as he opened his slacks and stepped out of them. Then Darnell scooped her up in one fluid motion and carried her into the bedroom where he placed her lightly on top of the bed. She leaned on an elbow and watched as he removed the rest of his clothes.

He had a beautiful body. It wasn't overly muscled, but hard and lean in all the right places. Claudia hated muscle-bound men who looked more like the Michelin Man caricature than human. Darnell's working as a weight trainer in a gym certainly had its compensations. The only thing her brain registered as she fixated on his gorgeous body was how good that beautiful big cock of his was going to feel deep inside of her. She never kidded herself. Big cocks were always better. In fact, the bigger the better was her motto. She preferred having trouble getting all of it into her snatch than wishing she could feel the damn thing. From what she could see, this guy was going to be just perfect.

Darnell didn't need a roadmap to find his way around her body. He knew exactly where he was heading. Standing at the foot of her bed he rolled her over onto her belly. Then he pulled her closer to the edge of the bed where he stood. She lifted up her rump, resting on her hands and knees, offering herself to him. He pushed his right thumb into her ass before he thrust most of his big, beautiful cock into her pussy. With the thumb and forefinger of his other hand, he kneaded Claudia's left nipple and began to rock her world.

As he pumped into her, Claudia rubbed and stroked her clit ratcheting up the tension. Darnell moved slowly at first, but it wasn't long before he was going as fast as he could, their bodies slapping together. She kept up with him, enjoying the ride. However, it wasn't long before she could feel the beginnings of an orgasm. Not wanting to surrender to it until the last moment, she allowed the tension to build like the torque on an engine. However, the way that boy was doing her, the first wave of spasms grabbed her, making her a very vocal goner.

"That's it baby girl. Let it all out," he said, just as he let himself go.

They cuddled together while their vitals slowed back down to normal. Darnell was a nice guy and she liked him. They'd met at the University of Pennsylvania last week. He had registered for a course in CPR and couldn't find the building where it was being held. Lost, he somehow ended up in the building where Claudia taught. Her class had ended and Darnell caught her heading to the cafeteria for some lunch. She found herself very attracted to him. They started talking and one thing eventually led to another.

She didn't see him as a potential relationship. That was the last thing Claudia desired.

She wasn't going to put herself in harm's way and let another man hurt her. The very fact that she had been able to allow men back into her life to fill her basic sexual needs had been a giant step. However, she had no intention of jeopardizing her progress by going out with a man more than once. Claudia was the original *no strings—no attachment* girl.

"How's about an *erotic* shower?" Darnell suggested.

"All right." Sex was a messy thing with all those drippy bodily fluids, so Claudia was all for that. It was the golden shower that she tended to avoid.

She led the way into her bathroom which, thank goodness, was large enough to be occupied by more than one person. Grabbing two fresh bath towels from her linen cabinet, Claudia slid open the glass doors and turned the water spigot on. Another thing which she was most thankful for was plentiful hot water. As she was adjusting the temperature, he ran his hands down over her body keeping her internal engine purring. When the water felt right, she stepped inside and Darnell followed, sliding the door closed behind them.

Once inside, he soaped up his hands and began to wash her breasts. The feeling of his hands on her skin began to excite her, pushing the needle on her passion barometer up. Claudia wanted to return the favor and turned around to soap Darnell's body, as well. Starting with his wide chest, she kneaded his man-buds with her soapy fingertips. They turned out to be sensitive and Darnell groaned. Emboldened by his reaction, she worked her way down to his cock which was now hard. She applied soap to his balls and adorable butt before she paid homage to his beautiful instrument of pleasure.

Even while Claudia lathered Darnell's gorgeous body, he continued to wash hers, as well. He was erotically soaping every conceivable—and inconceivable—spot on the front of her body driving her wild. However, when he went down on his knees and opened the folds of her sex, tonguing her from one end of her pussy to the other before latching his lips onto her clitoris, she wanted him so badly, she thought she'd die. She was literally about to beg him to thrust that beautiful cock into her pussy when he turned her around to face the tiles. He slipped two of his fingers inside her dripping pussy. Instinctively, she roughly rubbed herself against his fingers. That's when Darnell spread her ass-cheeks and began to lick her a-hole. No one had ever done this to her before. Between that and the fact his fingers felt like a cock, she was able to reach another earth-shattering climax.

When she was finished with her last spasm, he lifted her up slightly against the tiles and entered her pussy. It felt absolutely wonderful. Holding her against the wall of the shower, he pumped into her until she felt him stiffen and then come. He let her down and the water cascaded down over them both, washing them clean.

About this time they both began to resemble a pair of dried prunes, so it was time to get out of the shower. They toweled dry and headed towards the bed. Originally, she hadn't planned on him staying the night. However, he worked so hard, she didn't have the heart to throw him out. Claudia was exhausted herself and within minutes of placing her head down on the pillow, she was out for the count.

When she opened her eyes the next morning, which was Sunday, he was gone. He'd left a note explaining that he had several appointments at the gym and would call during the week. Claudia dreaded that phone call. She didn't want to have to tell him that, though he'd been a wonderful lay, she didn't want to see him again. That part was always the stickiest and was never easy. Men didn't take rejection well. However, women took longer to recover from rejection. She'd been a prime example. And the man who had rejected her was a jerk named Jerome.

She'd been seeing Jerome for more than two years. He'd spent a lot of time dogging her for some kind of commitment. Just as she was about to tell him yes to their moving in together, the unthinkable happened. Claudia had spent the night at his place but left early the next day to pick up some papers from her office.. Half-way to work, she'd realized she'd left her cell phone on the nightstand in the bedroom. When she returned to the apartment, she let herself in with the key Jerome had given her. She found his buxom next-door neighbor riding him as if he were a prize stallion.

So much for commitment.

The shock was overwhelming, since she had thought he was happy with the relationship. She certainly had been. What upset her the most was the fact she never saw this coming. She was now more vigilant and wiser, and she vowed never to allow something like that ever happen to her again. Claudia made up her mind then to go back to school, get a degree and become independent. She would never again rely on anyone but herself.

Because most people tended to look at her self-preservation program as a way of running away from reality, or worse, just a form of eccentricity, Claudia kept her personal and professional lives separate. She never dated anyone from the teaching staff or administration at the university. This in itself earned her the nicknames, *The Iron Maiden* or The *Frost Queen*. If that was the price she'd have to pay in order to keep her heart safe, so be it. It was her life and she could do whatever she damned well please with it, anyway. They didn't know her or why she chose to travel down this path. And she intended to keep it that way.

Things ended up working out just fine for her. She applied to the University of Pennsylvania right after she discovered Jerome's infidelity and put herself through school. Deciding on becoming an English professor, she continued on to grad school while she worked as a teaching assistant. Claudia landed a job as an assistant professor and finally a professor. Now at the age of thirty-five, she was in line to become the next head of the English department. Claudia had no husband or family to vie for her time, so she was able to put most of her energy into teaching. When she felt the urge for sex, she merely went out on a date. An attractive woman with a lithe body and exotic, high cheek bones, she was never at a loss for dates. Her lifestyle may not work for everyone; however, it worked for her. That's why she braced herself for the awful conversation that would eventually come when Darnell called her back to make another date.

About the Author

With nearly 200 short stories, numerous anthologies, novellas and novels in print, whether she's writing spicy hot erotica as Candy Caine or less edgy contemporary romance as her alter ego, Candace Gold, she keeps her husband, Robert, on his toes in their Arizona home. Supportive with her writing career, he's always willing to help her add authenticity to the scenes in her stories. After all, technique is so important for good writing. When asked why she began to write, Candy says: "Reading has always been an addiction for me and my biggest thrill is to bring the joy of reading to others. That's what writing is all about."

http://www.candycaine.com

If you enjoyed this eBook you might also enjoy these...

SEXY, FABULOUS E-BOOKS BY CANDY CAINE

Christmas with a Stranger

Two days before Christmas, sassy Allie Benson found herself stranded in a wintry wilderness with wealthy, sexy, Roy Colby. Staying warm was a priority. But the heat their bodies generated went way beyond what either of them had ever dreamed.

Dangerous Attractions

Kayla Jackson had everything a lover of a rich man could have—jewels, security, a life in the fast track. It was madness then for her to act on her overwhelming attraction to her lover's assistant, no matter how hot he was.

Forever Yours

Jade Green couldn't be happier hanging out with her friend, Charles. It was a low maintenance relationship—no intimacy, no drama. She never dreamed Charles had other plans.

It's Love That Really Counts

If you had to choose between your family and your last chance at love—which would you choose?

Love with a Younger Man

Amber was sick of playing second fiddle to her boyfriend's business deals. So she decided to "cougar" it with a blue-eyed hunk of masculinity. She never dreamed her hidden past would come back to haunt her and threaten the love she found with her young lover.

Never is Not Forever

Claudia Brown didn't want marriage. But she wanted a baby. So she set out to find the perfect sperm donor—someone who wouldn't be around later to even know he had fathered a child. Falling in love with the man was not in the game plan.